To:

From:

Given on this date:

Text written by Tim Wesemann.
Illustrations by Dennis Edwards.

Character ownership and licensing by P23 Entertainment Inc.
This book is published in association with Nappaland Literary Agency, an independent agency dedicated to publishing works that are: Authentic. Relevant. Eternal. Visit us on the web at http://www.Nappaland. com.

ISBN: 978-1-5359-2372-9
Dewey Decimal Classification: C220.95
Subject Heading: BIBLE STORIES \ HEROES AND HEROINES

 Printed in Shenzhen, Guangdong, China in June 2018.
1 2 3 4 5 6 7 8 22 21 20 19 18

BIBLEMAN DEVOTIONAL

written by

Tim Wesemann

illustrations by

Dennis Edwards

B&H KIDS
Nashville, Tennessee

CONTENTS

THE ARMOR OF GOD

Finally, be strengthened by the Lord and by his vast strength. Put on the full armor of God so that you can stand against the schemes of the devil. For our struggle is not against flesh and blood, but against the rulers, against the authorities, against the cosmic powers of this darkness, against evil, spiritual forces in the heavens. For this reason take up the full armor of God, so that you may be able to resist in the evil day, and having prepared everything, to take your stand. Stand, therefore, with truth like a belt around your waist, righteousness like armor on your chest, and your feet sandaled with readiness for the gospel of peace. In every situation take up the shield of faith with which you can extinguish all the flaming arrows of the evil one. Take the helmet of salvation and the sword of the Spirit—which is the word of God.

—Ephesians 6:10–17

Meet the Bibleteam!

Bibleman

Josh Carpenter

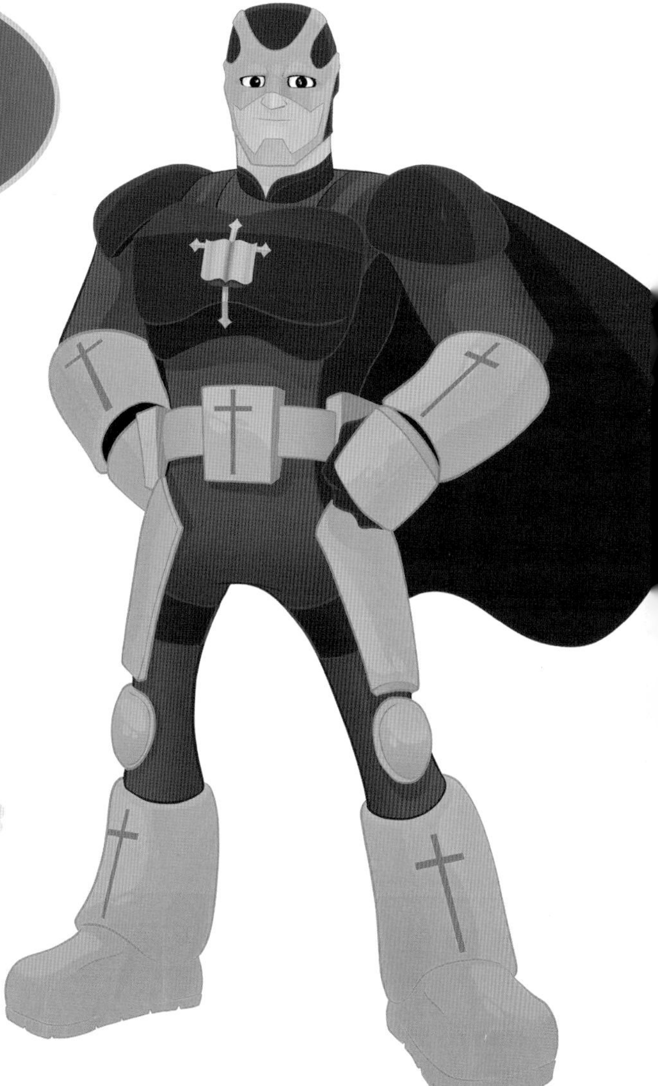

MY GOAL: To lead kids to Jesus Christ.

TACTICS: I teach Bible stories that relate to kids' situations, and I defeat villains with Scripture.

FAVE SCRIPTURE:
Ephesians 6:10–17

WEAPON OF CHOICE:
The sword of the Spirit (the Word of God)

HOBBY: Riding motorcycles

FAVE SLUSH-EZ FLAVOR:
Bubblegum-java-mint

Biblegirl

Lia Martin

MY GOAL: To protect kids from the enemies of God!

TACTICS: I develop Bible lessons, and I oppose villains.

FAVE SCRIPTURE:
Philippians 4:8–9

WEAPON OF CHOICE:
Dual light-tonfas (used with God's Word)

HOBBY: Music and singing

FAVE SLUSH-EZ FLAVOR:
Strawberry-chocolate

Cypher

Kerry Turner, "KT"

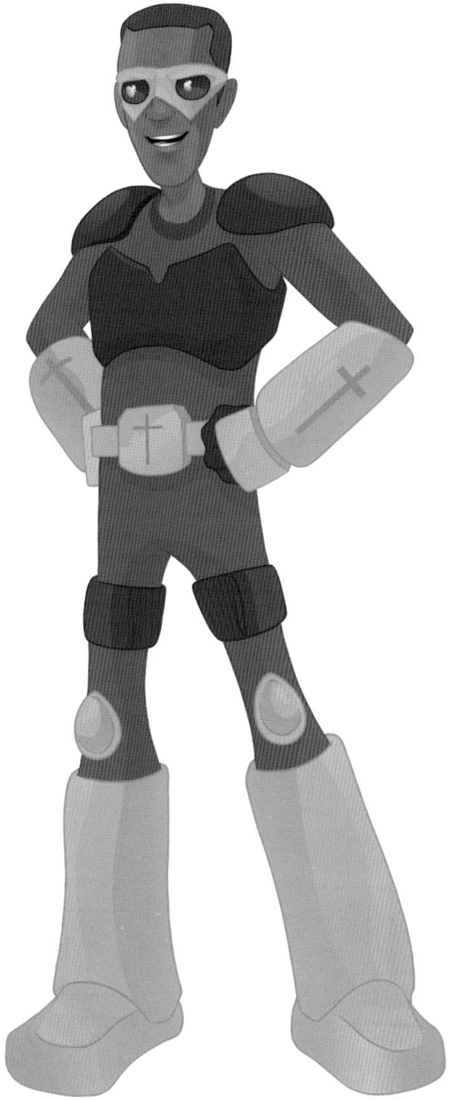

MY GOAL: To help kids live for Jesus Christ.

TACTICS: I use innovative media and technology to defeat villains.

FAVE SCRIPTURE:
2 Timothy 2:15

WEAPON OF CHOICE:
Light-bo staff (used with God's Word)

HOBBY: Writing computer code and tweaking processors

FAVE SLUSH-EZ FLAVOR:
Cantaloupe-bubblegum

Melody

MY GOAL: **To help advance the Bibleteam's mission.**

TACTICS: **As a rookie, I assist the Bibleteam with vehicle operation and technology monitoring.**

FAVE SCRIPTURE:
Colossians 3:23–25

WEAPON OF CHOICE:
Dual light-escrima (used with God's Word)

HOBBY: **Gymnastics**

FAVE SLUSH-EZ FLAVOR:
Kiwi-lemon swirl

Bibleman!

The Official Theme Song

Bibleman! Bibleman!
Fighting for the way, he's the Bibleman.

Bibleman! Fighting the good fight,
Taking the shield of faith and the belt of truth,
Bibleman is on the move.
The sword of the Spirit is the Word of God.
There's nothing it can't do.

Bibleman! Bibleman!
Fighting the good fight,
Wearing the breastplate of righteousness
and the helmet of salvation.
Biblegirl, Cypher, and Melody—
Fighting for the way.

We stand together in the sight of God.
We stand together to do what's right.

Bibleman! Bibleman!
Fighting for God's truth and way!

Week 1

Taking Out Slacker and the Trash

Power Bible Verse

I will forgive their wrongdoing, and I will never again remember their sins.—Hebrews 8:12

Slacker was happy as he lay in the recliner in front of the TV with a bag of chips. He convinced Stu, who was stretched out on the sofa next to him, not to take out the trash like his dad had asked him to do.

Biblegirl received a threat report from Cypher that the chip-eating Slacker had made himself comfortable at Stu's house. The tracker showed no movement, which was Slacker's favorite activity!

Biblegirl jumped into action, flew to Stu's, grabbed the chips out of Slacker's hands, and took a bite out of his evil plan for Stu. Biblegirl talked to Stu about the importance of listening to his parents, doing what they asked, asking for forgiveness when he didn't, and always doing his best.

Then she shared an idea with Stu. "Think about the trash as though it's a pile of things you do wrong—when you sin against God and others. As you carry it to the curb, ask Jesus for forgiveness for your sin-trash. Jesus takes that sin away. He takes that trash out of your life and sends it away for good!"

When Biblegirl left she handed Stu a card. It read, "I will forgive their wrongdoing, and I will never again remember their sins.—Hebrews 8:12."

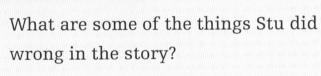

LET'S TALK

What are some of the things Stu did wrong in the story?

Why is it important and right for us to listen to our parents when they ask us to do something?

It's amazing that when God forgives our sins He forgets them! He throws them out like the trash. How does that change the way you forgive someone?

Optional: What are your favorite snacks when you're hanging out?

Power Word of the Week: FORGIVENESS

Bibleteam Challenge

Offer to take the trash out this week (if you don't already). Think about Biblegirl's sin-trash lesson as you do. On a small piece of paper write (or have someone write for you), "I am forgiven," and tape it to the trashcan in your room. When you throw trash into it, you can remember God forgives and forgets. He removes our sin—trash.

LET'S PRAY TOGETHER

Dear Jesus, I will spend my life thanking You for Your forgiveness and love for me. I don't deserve it. I don't understand it. But I accept it. It changes the way I live and forgive. Thank You, Jesus. Amen.

Week 2
From Selfish and Smad to Glad

Power Bible Verse

"Whoever welcomes one little child such as this in my name welcomes me."
—Mark 9:37

Maddie was kinda sad and kinda mad; she was smad! Her parents surprised her with an "I'm a Big Sister" T-shirt. A baby brother was coming soon! So why was Maddie smad?

The Sultan of Selfishness told Maddie that a new baby wasn't good news. A baby meant her parents would pay more attention to him. He'd get lots of presents, and she'd only get a few. Everyone would think he was so adorable, forgetting she was super cute years before he was born.

He'll burp, and adults will laugh, she thought, *but if I do that, they'll say I'm not polite. He'll cry, and they'll hold and hug him. If I cry, they'll say I'm fine.* Maddie needed to know she was the most important kid in the house. That's why Maddie was smad.

But when Biblegirl and Melody showed up, they used God's Word to fight off the selfish enemy. They told Maddie that Philippians 2:3 says, "in humility consider others as more important than yourselves." They said Jesus would love her and her brother the same. With Maddie and her parents' help, God would take care of her brother, teach him, and make sure he loves Jesus just like she does.

Suddenly smad Maddie turned into glad Maddie!

LET'S TALK

What are some things you've been selfish about this week? Did anything or anyone make you smad (sad+mad) this week? What changed those feelings?

What does it mean to be selfless? Is it hard for you to act selfless?

What do you enjoy doing with your brother or sister (or friends)? In what ways do you help each other?

Power Word of the Week: *SELFLESS*

Bibleteam Challenge

Think of selfless ways you can help your family or friends. But don't just think about ways, do the kind act you've thought about.

LET'S PRAY TOGETHER

Jesus, You were selfless when You died on the cross and took our sins in our place. You did it because You love us perfectly. And You give back forgiveness and an unending life with You. I want to think and act like You every day. Help me, please. Thank You, Jesus. Amen.

Week 3
Sour Note Sends Baroness Away

Power Bible Verse

Trust in the LORD with all your heart, and do not rely on your own understanding.—Proverbs 3:5

The Baroness Fitzhugh-Ferguson promised some families she would teach their kids music. She tapped her conflict crystal stick to get their attention. Starting with a song her mother taught her when she was a little girl, she had them sing:

> I am trusting me, Lord Jesus, trusting only me.
> Trusting me for no forgiveness; let's agree!

The kids stopped singing and started arguing, "Those aren't the right words!" "The Baroness says they're right, so sing!" "Cooper can't sing!" "*You* can't, Emma!" "No forgiveness? Trusting me? What?" Now everyone was upset.

Melody heard the commotion while riding by in the Biblevan and rushed inside. Melody realized the Baroness had made the kids argue with her lies! On that sour note, Melody sent the Baroness packing. Then she taught the kids new, better words to the song:

I am trusting Thee, Lord, Jesus; trusting only Thee.
Trusting Thee for full forgiveness, sure and free!

LET'S TALK

Besides Jesus, who do you trust the most? Why?

Why do you think we often trust ourselves more than anyone else?

What is it about Jesus that makes us want to trust Him more than anyone or anything?

Optional: What are some things we trust?

Power Word of the Week: TRUST

Bibleteam Challenge

First, sing Melody's song in the devotion—not the Baroness's! Play a trust game with one or more family members or friends. Blindfold one person and ask the others to lead them around the room or house with just their voice. Take turns and see if you learned anything about trust.

LET'S PRAY TOGETHER

Holy Spirit, teach me to trust in the Lord with all my heart, instead of relying on my own under-standing. In all my ways I want to know Him. He will make my paths straight. I pray this trusting Thee, Lord Jesus. Amen.

Week 4
The Grand Duchess of Greed and Miss Iwanna Havit

Power Bible Verse

A greedy person stirs up conflict, but whoever trusts in the LORD will prosper.—Proverbs 28:25

Mr. and Mrs. Havit received a very strange but important-looking email. It said the Havit's should change their daughter's name from *Lana* to *Iwanna*. When they saw who sent it, they immediately forwarded it to the Bibleteam and talked with their daughter. And when Lana's parents read her the email, she yelled, "I wanna know who sent that!"

"It's from the Grand Duchess of Greed," her dad replied. Lana didn't understand, but her parents did. Her mother explained. "If you changed your name, it would be Iwanna Havit." Then she repeated it slowly. "I wanna have it. Do you understand? You do say that a lot, Lana. 'I wanna have this and that. I wanna have it now!' You've been wanting so many things you don't need. That's called greed. You've been thinking about yourself and not others. You made the Grand Duchess of Greed happy! But is that how you want to act as God's child?" her mom continued. "We can be content, happy with what we have. God has blessed us with so much, especially the gift of Jesus. He'd love for all of us to say, 'I wanna know Jesus better,' instead of, 'I wanna have it—have everything.'"

Bibleman sent an email to the Havit family. It read: Jesus said, "Watch out and be on guard against all greed, because one's life is not in the abundance of his possessions." —Luke 12:15.

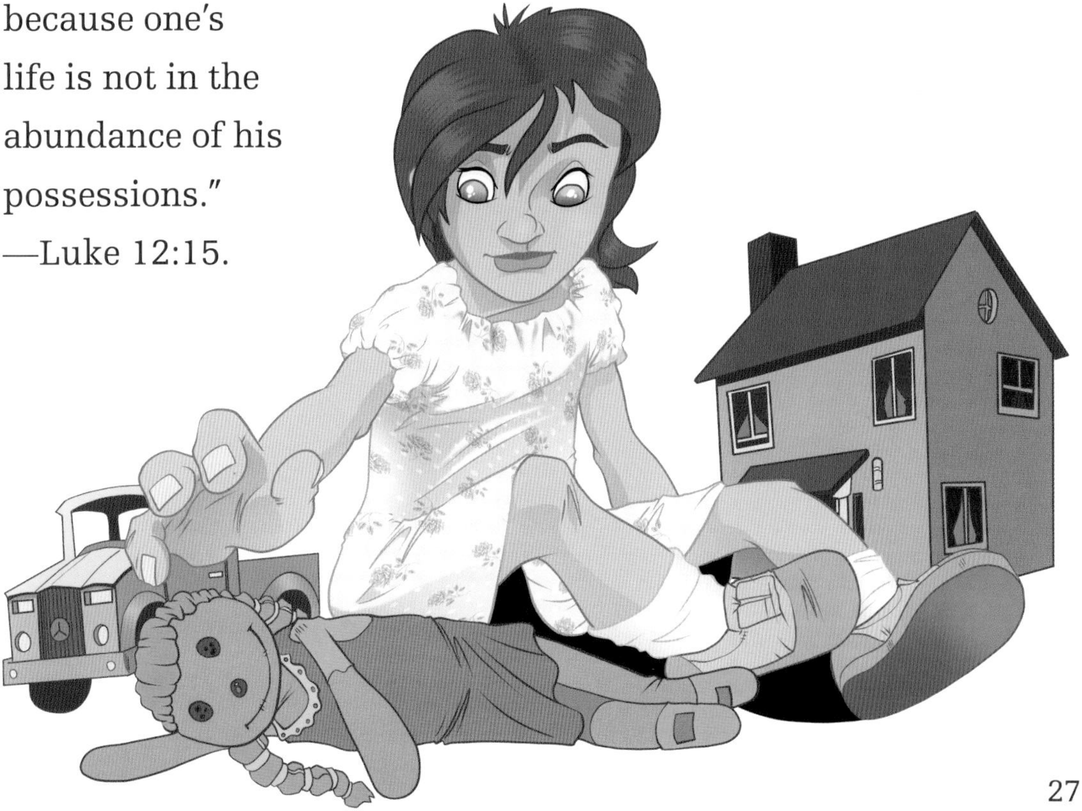

LET'S TALK

Talk with your parent or another adult about what it means to be content.

When were some times last week that you said, "I wanna . . . ."?

If you say, "I wanna know Jesus better," how do you think you could make that happen?

Power Word of the Week: CONTENT

Bibleteam Challenge

Share toys or clothes with other kids who don't have as many as you. Your parents can help you find a place to donate them. Also, say to your parents, "I wanna thank you for not naming me Iwanna Havit!" (If that happens to be your name, well, I wanna tell you I'm sorry!)

LET'S PRAY TOGETHER

Jesus, I wanna know You better. I wanna learn how to be content and thankful. I wanna thank You for helping me. In Your name I pray. Amen.

Week 5

Bibleman Cleans Up Room 1427

Power Bible Verse

"Peace I leave with you. My peace I give to you. I do not give to you as the world gives. Don't let your heart be troubled or fearful."

—John 14:27

Dr. Fear had an evil plan ready for John and Dominic at Grace N. Mercy Children's Hospital.

Dr. Fear pretended to clean John's room. He used a bottle of Fear-It spray to wipe away dirt and germs. Suddenly John became scared and worried about his operation and getting better.

Dominic wanted to visit his friend John at the hospital but was afraid he wouldn't know what to say to him. Dominic's dad waited in the hallway while Dominic went to visit John. Before he opened the door Dominic took a deep breath and stuck his hand in his coat pocket. To his surprise he found a note in his pocket. It read, "Remember this, Dominic: The Lord said to Moses in Exodus 4:12, 'I will help you speak and I will teach you what to say.'" It was signed, Bibleman.

Dominic looked at John's room number and smiled: 1427. He remembered what Jesus said to His friends in John 14:27. He shared it with his friend, John: "Jesus said, 'Peace I leave with you. My peace I give to you.'" With that, the Fear-It changed to Cheer-It, and Jesus' peace filled John's heart, putting an end to Dr. Fear's attack.

LET'S TALK

How would you feel about visiting a sick friend? What might you be afraid of?

How do you think Moses felt after the Lord told him He would help him and teach him what to say?

Describe peace. What is it like to feel really peaceful?

Power Word of the Week: PEACE

Bibleteam Challenge

Memorize the words Jesus told His close friends in John 14:27—"Peace I leave with you. My peace I give to you."

LET'S PRAY TOGETHER

Give me peace, Jesus. Your peace. I worry too much. I'm afraid. I get upset. I need Your peace. And help me bring Your peace to others to help them wipe away any fear. Thank You, Jesus. Amen.

Week 6

Lemonade and Sweet News

Power Bible Verse

Now faith is the reality of what is hoped for, the proof of what is not seen. —Hebrews 11:1

The Mayor of Maybe looked outside and spotted Amy and Jessica carrying a sign that read: *Bibleteam approved lemonade: 5 cents! All money helps buy Bibleman Bible Storybooks 4 sick children!*

The crabby mayor stomped over to the two girls. "Bible storybooks?" he grumbled. "What if God isn't real? Have you ever seen Jesus?"

Amy whispered to Jessica, "The Bibleteam told me what to say." She bravely spoke up. "Have you ever seen your brain, your heart, or your lungs? No? But you know they keep you alive! You believe, even though you haven't seen.

That's faith. We know God's truth. We trust in what the Bible says. By faith we know Jesus gave His life for us on the cross, rose from the dead, and lives. By faith we believe in His promises, forgiveness, heaven, love, and so much more."

The mayor muttered something and left. Jessica called out, "Would you like some free lemonade? It has some sugar in it you can't see. You'll just have to believe it's there!"

LET'S TALK

If someone asked you what faith is, what would you tell them?

Who do you know who has a very strong faith in Jesus?

How does the Holy Spirit help grow our faith stronger and stronger?

Optional: Read the story of Jesus and his close friend, Peter, walking on the lake in Matthew 14:22–33. Talk about the faith shown in that story. Would you have done what Peter did? You may want to act out the story.

Power Word of the Week:

FAITH

Bibleteam Challenge

Give someone in your family something you have that is very special or important and ask them to keep it for you for one week. Tell them you have faith in them to keep it safe. When you get it back, talk about having faith in or trusting that person and the difference between that and having faith in God.

LET'S PRAY TOGETHER

Thank You, Holy Spirit, for creating faith within me. I believe the Bible is true. I believe in God the Father, Son, and Holy Spirit! I know Jesus rescued me from my sins and loves me! Amen.

Week 7

Where Do You Live?

Power Bible Verse

"A thief comes only to steal and kill and destroy. I have come so that they may have life and have it in abundance."
—John 10:10

Nooooo!" the Empress of Unhappiness shouted when she looked up at the street sign. *Smile Street*. "Why? Why? Why would anyone want to live here? I must change this." Her timing was perfect. It was Sunday morning. Many families would be at church. *They're probably talking and singing about joyful things like hope, forgiveness, and God's love*, she thought. *Enough!*

The Empress had a wicked plan. First, she would rename the street *Dismal Dead End*. She'd paint houses blue and their rooms a shade of gloom. Adding boring flooring sounded about right. Unhappy, sappy syrup would fill kitchen shelves, and sad sacks of potatoes went into bins. And by using down pillows, families would fall asleep feeling down and wake depressed.

But the Empress didn't plan on Melody driving down Smile Street after church. Melody alerted headquarters of the situation, reporting she'd handle the evil plan. She jumped out of the Biblevan and pointed her dual-light escrima stick at the villain. "Empress, I'm sure you have an evil plan for Smile Street. Be gone! And remember, John 10:10 tells us that Jesus said, 'A thief comes only to steal and kill and destroy. I have come so that they may have life and have it in abundance.' Joy lives here because of Jesus!"

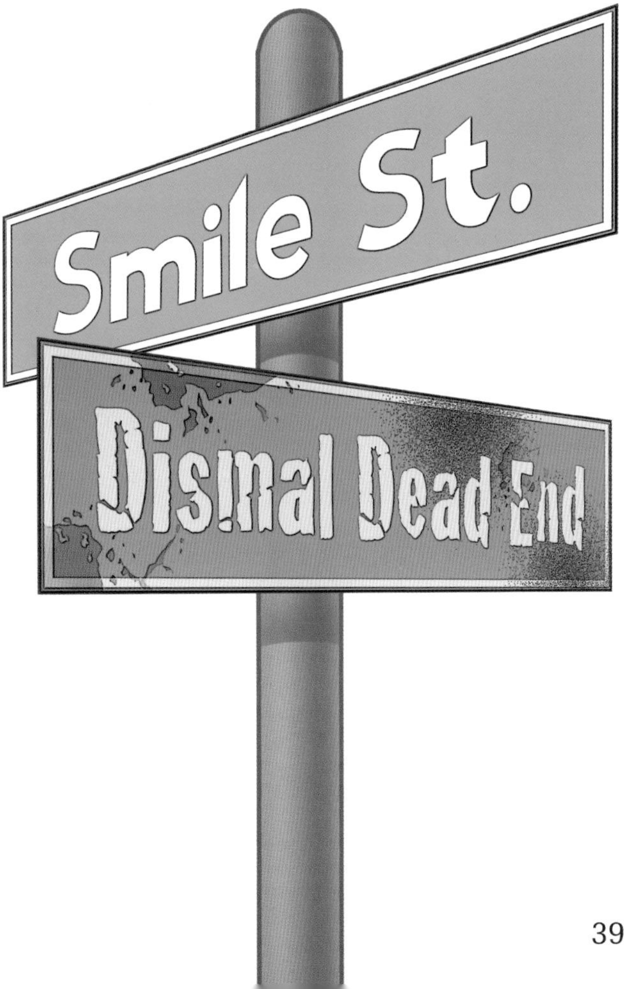

LET'S TALK

Do you live on a street with people who love Jesus?

Who are some of the happiest, nicest Christians you know? Have you thanked them for sharing their smiles and the joy of Jesus with you?

Jesus gives an abundant life. What does that mean?

Power Word of the Week: LIFE

Bibleteam Challenge

Try to smile and say "Hi" to people you see in your neighborhood, school, or city. Notice how people respond. A simple smile and kind word can make a big difference in someone's life.

LET'S PRAY TOGETHER

Jesus, the promises in Your Word bring me joy. Knowing You are always present with me makes me happy. Help me share this joy with strangers and people I know. I hope they see You though my joy. Amen.

Week 8

A Prescription for Patience

Power Bible Verse

Love is patient, love is kind.
—1 Corinthians 13:4

Marco and his mom sat in the doctor's waiting room. The doctor was late because of an emergency. Marco felt like they had been waiting for soooo long. Waiting, waiting, and more waiting. Marco didn't notice the Whiner Brothers sitting next to him. They hid their faces, pretending to read magazines. They showed up to make things painful for Marco, his mom, and everyone else there.

The Whiner Brothers whispered so only Marco would hear them. They said things like, "Complain about how long you've been waiting." So Marco did. "Stand up and loudly tell your mom you want to leave and come another time." Marco did. "Stomp your feet." He did that too.

Each time his mother asked him not to talk so rudely

and to wait patiently. "You're being a very impatient patient," his mother told him.

Suddenly, out of nowhere, Biblegirl ran in and pulled the magazines away from the Whiner Brothers, took them by their collars, and kicked them out of the office. She turned back and said, "Yes, I have power, but here's a prescription for wisdom from God in Proverbs 16:32: Patience is better than power."

Marco told everyone in the room that he was sorry for the way he acted. "I'll try to be a patient patient from now on," Marco said with a smile.

LET'S TALK

Do you find it easy or difficult to be patient? Where is the most difficult place for you to be patient?

When you're not patient, the easiest thing to do is get upset. God's enemy loves for us to get upset and mad. What might help you to stay patient and kind?

Do you think it's hard for God to be patient with us?

Optional: Do you think memorizing this week's key verse can help us if we say it over and over when we're not patient?

Power Word of the Week: PATIENCE

Bibleteam Challenge

Write (or have someone help you write) a prayer asking for patience.

LET'S PRAY TOGETHER

Pray the prayer you wrote or if you haven't written it yet, pray a prayer with your own words.

Week 9

Was It a Dream?

Power Bible Verse

All Scripture is inspired by God and is profitable for teaching, for rebuking, for correcting, for training in righteousness, so that the man of God may be complete, equipped for every good work.—2 Timothy 3:16–17

Sully ran to tell his parents he met the Bibleteam in their headquarters. Well, it was a dream, but it seemed real! He saw computers, tablets, and gizmos that Cypher used to track down villains. Melody showed him the super cool Biblevan. Bibleman and Biblegirl showed him the room where they pray and study the Bible.

Sully saw three posters on the wall that remind the team of God's power, the Bible, and the love of Jesus. One poster showed the armor of God from Ephesians 6:10–17. Another read, "'Lord, to whom will we go? You have the words of eternal life.'—John 6:68." And the third poster read, "'For God loved the world in this way: He gave his one and only Son, so that everyone who believes in him will not perish but have eternal life.'—John 3:16."

"Then I high-fived Bibleman, and . . . and I woke up!" Sully told his parents. "Can you please help me make a Bible verse poster for my room?"

LET'S TALK

If you had a dream about the Bibleteam headquarters what would it look like?

Scripture is another word for the Bible or God's Word. Why is it important to believe all of Scripture is true and from God?

This week's key verse tells a lot about what the Bibleteam does and believes. Have someone explain the meaning and big words you may not understand.

Power Word of the Week: SCRIPTURE

Bibleteam Challenge

Work with a family member and make a Bible verse picture or poster for your room. Choose a Bible verse and write it on paper or poster board. Draw and color pictures of the Bibleteam (or whatever you like) to decorate it.

LET'S PRAY TOGETHER

Scripture, Your Word, is so important. Your Word is truth. As I grow, help me to read it, understand it, love it, trust it, and share it with others. And thank You for the Bibleteam ministry. Help them to bring kids to Christ and defeat enemies. In Jesus' name. Amen.

Week 10
The Hunt for Golden Eggs and Good News

Power Bible Verse

He is not here. For he has risen, just as he said. Come and see the place where he lay.—Matthew 28:6

Connor knew absolutely, positively, no-doubt-about-it surely that Easter was all about eggs and candy and presents! But he didn't know he was under attack from the Ambassador of Ignorance, who didn't want Connor to go to the Bibleteam's Easter egg hunt and find out differently. Since a friend invited him, the Ambassador lost out, and Connor went anyway.

Bibleman welcomed the kids and shouted, "Happy Easter! Happy Resurrection Day!" Biblegirl told the kids about one special golden egg. Whoever found it would find very good news inside! The kids darted off, filling their baskets with eggs. Cypher set up an invisible defense fence, keeping enemies like the Ambassador of Ignorance away.

Soon everyone heard Connor scream, "YESSSS! I FOUND THE GOLDEN EGG!" He ran to the Bibleteam. Everyone watched Connor open the egg and heard him shout, "NOOOO! IT'S EMPTY!"

Bibleman explained that the empty egg contained the joy-filled good news that Jesus lives, even though He died.

Melody told the kids Easter eggs can remind them of new life, and candy is like the sweet, good news that Jesus lives. What a great Easter present! Because Jesus lives we can live forever with Him! Connor shouted, "OHHH! Jesus' empty grave fills us with sweet, good news. Jesus lives! So that's what Easter is all about!"

LET'S TALK

What is Easter? What do you like about Easter?

Why is the news that Jesus lives so very, very important?

In what special ways do your church and family celebrate Easter—Resurrection Day?

Power Word of the Week: RESURRECTION

Bibleteam Challenge

During the coming week have a small Easter celebration with your family. It doesn't have to be Easter to celebrate that Jesus lives!

LET'S PRAY TOGETHER

Dear living Jesus, Your resurrection news changes everything. Your empty grave fills us with the sweet, good news that You are alive. What a happy day we can celebrate every day of the year!
Amen.

Week 11

Let's Tell the World!

Power Bible Verse

How is it that each of us can hear them in our own native language? —Acts 2:8

Cypher and Melody were surrounded by computer parts. They had created a device the Bibleteam could use to defeat their enemies and help kids who didn't speak English. The team could share God's Word and good news with the kids in a language they understood!

Now they were ready to test it. Cypher programmed it to say, "'Go, therefore, and make disciples of all nations.'—Matthew 28:19," in Spanish. Melody pushed the button on her armor, and a voice said, "Necesito usar el baño."

"Nooo! That's not right," Cypher groaned. That's Spanish for I need to use the bathroom. Let's get back to work. We can make this right with God's help."

They tried it again a week later. Cypher pushed the button on the armor and said, "Read Romans 8:31 in Bosnian." A voice from the speaker said, "Ako je Bog za nas, ko je protiv nas?"

"Woohoo! That's right! 'If God is for us, who is against us?' We did it! God did it! Now we can help so many more kids defeat the enemy. We can share the good news that Jesus rescued us, loves us, and forgives us in any language!"

LET'S TALK

Do you know kids who speak languages other than English?

Have an adult read Acts 2:1–12 with you and talk about the miracle that happened on the day we call Pentecost.

Pray for missionaries in other countries. Ask your pastor for the name of a missionary your family can help or pray for during the year.

Power Word of the Week: LANGUAGES

Bibleteam Challenge

With an adult helping you on the computer, learn to say *Jesus loves you* in some different languages, including American Sign Language.

LET'S PRAY TOGETHER

Heavenly Father, thank You for computers, gizmos, and all sorts of ways to tell people all over the world about Your love. Bless the people who are able to create programs like that. Let's tell the world of Your love and gifts. In Jesus' name, amen.

Week 12

Kindness through the Roof

Power Bible Verse

The fruit of the Spirit is love, joy, peace, patience, kindness, goodness, faithfulness, gentleness, and self-control.
—Galatians 5:22–23

Biblegirl loved using the Bible's lessons to teach kids about Jesus! She was so excited to share one of her favorite lessons in Mark 2 that tells about the kindness of five men, one named Jesus.

"It begins with a man who could not walk. Instead, he lay on a mat with a pole along each side. He couldn't go anywhere unless four people lifted the poles and carried him."

"One day four men were very kind to him. They carried the man on his mat to see Jesus. They believed Jesus could heal his legs so he could walk. When they got to the house where Jesus was, it was so full that people were standing outside. They couldn't get close to Jesus! But they had an idea. They would carry the man on his mat up a ladder to the roof. Then they'd make a hole in the roof and use rope to lower him down to Jesus!"

"Their plan worked! And Jesus showed great kindness. When He saw that these men believed Jesus could heal, He did—in two ways! First, and more important, Jesus forgave the man's sins. Then Jesus told him to stand up, take his mat, and go home. He did! The people who saw him were so excited. They praised and thanked God in heaven for Jesus' amazing kindness."

"Now that you know about the great kindness of Jesus and the four men, you'll also want to bring others to Jesus," said Biblegirl.

LET'S TALK

If you were the man in that story, what four people might have shown you kindness and carried you to Jesus?

What's the kindest thing someone has done for you?

Why was Jesus forgiving the man's sin a greater miracle than healing him?

Power Word of the Week: KINDNESS

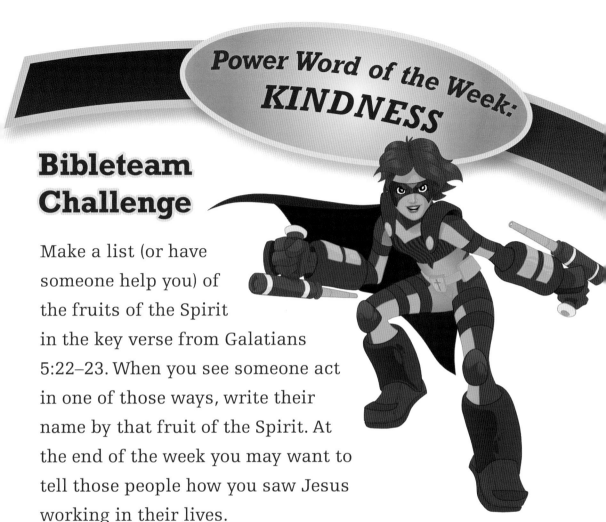

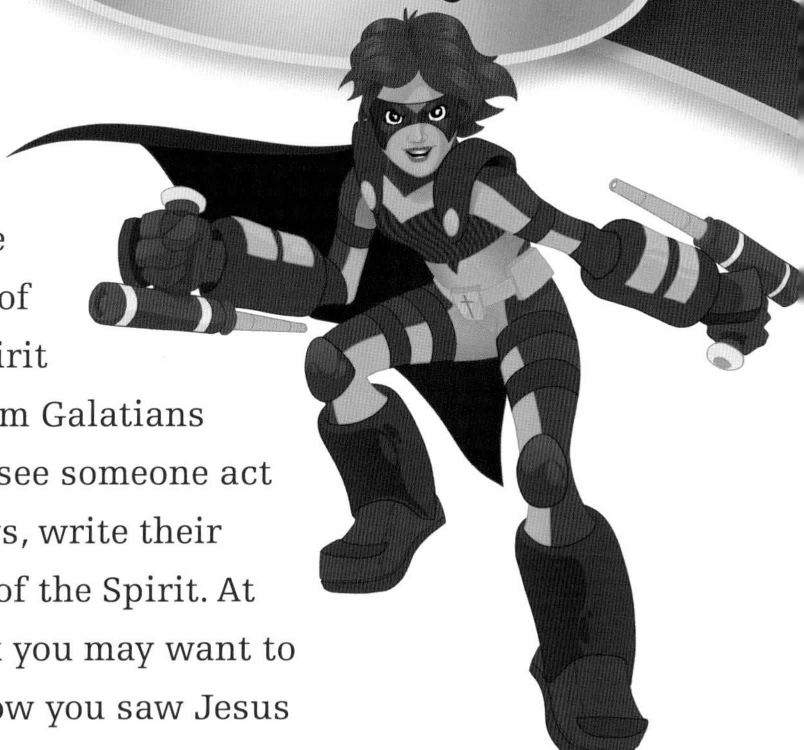

Bibleteam Challenge

Make a list (or have someone help you) of the fruits of the Spirit in the key verse from Galatians 5:22–23. When you see someone act in one of those ways, write their name by that fruit of the Spirit. At the end of the week you may want to tell those people how you saw Jesus working in their lives.

LET'S PRAY TOGETHER

Jesus, help me look for people who need help and kindness. Show me ways I can help them in a safe way. I want everyone around me to come to You. Thank You for the miracle of forgiving me through Your death and resurrection. In Your name I pray. Amen.

Week 13

The Lion, the Turtle, and the Cake

Power Bible Verse

Don't let your mouth speak dishonestly.—Proverbs 4:24

Bella had a dress-like-an-animal birthday party. One boy wore a turtleneck shirt and a shell on his back. Another carried a suitcase with an elephant trunk sticker. No one wanted to play games with the cheetah. One lion, two giraffes, three monkeys, and nineteen panda bears also came. Bella also invited Bibleman, who was dressed as . . . Bibleman, wearing the Armor of God.

A group of kid-animals threw candy at the balloons, trying to pop them. The boy-turtle heard a voice behind him say, "Kick the ball to pop a balloon." So he did. The ball missed the balloons, but landed on the birthday cake. What a mess!

Bella screamed! No one knew who kicked the ball. A voice whispered to turtle, "Don't say anything. They'll blame a monkey." So he didn't say anything, and they blamed a monkey.

But Bibleman knew what happened. The voice the turtle heard was the lion, Fibbler! Bibleman cornered him so he couldn't escape and asked the turtle to join them. Words appeared on Bibleman's Shield of Faith: "Don't let your mouth speak dishonestly—Proverbs 4:24."

The boy told Bibleman his mouth didn't speak dishonestly. He didn't say anything at all!

Bibleman explained that sometimes not saying anything can hurt others. The boy told Bella he was very sorry. And Bibleman sent Fibbler to buy a new birthday cake and a necklace for Bella that read, "Jesus loves you! That's the truth!"

LET'S TALK

The Fibbler loves when people get in trouble by lying. Name a time that happened to you.

The Fibbler was in a disguise in the story. How did Satan disguise himself in the Garden of Eden when he lied to trick Adam and Eve (Genesis 3:1)?

What is the best true news you've ever heard?

Optional: If you were at Bella's birthday party, what kind of animal would you have been? Why?

Power Word of the Week: HONESTY

Bibleteam Challenge

The next time your teacher or your parents ask you to tell the truth, do it. See if you feel their trust more after you do.

LET'S PRAY TOGETHER

Jesus, You love me, care for me, watch over me, forgive me, live for me, help me, bless me, and so much more! And that's the truth! That's great news! I'm so thankful, Jesus. Amen.

Week 14
Walking Paradise Path in Kingdom Park

Power Bible Verse

Jesus [said], "I am the way, the truth, and the life. No one comes to the Father except through me."
—John 14:6

Biblegirl noticed a family in Kingdom Park looking at the trail map. They couldn't decide which trail to hike. Biblegirl shared that her favorite trail was Paradise Path, the only one that would lead them to a hill with a cross and a beautiful view over the river.

Biblegirl knew this was a perfect time to share a Bible lesson with the family. She told them about Jesus talking to His close friends before His crucifixion and death. But Jesus didn't want them to be sad because He would come back to life three days later. And then He would go to heaven to prepare a place for them and all who follow and trust Jesus as the one who rescued people with forgiveness for their sins. Jesus wanted to make sure His friends would be with Him forever. They told Jesus they didn't know the way to where He was going. Jesus told them that He was the Way! Going to the cross and following Jesus was the only way to heaven.

"It's kind of like Kingdom Park," Biblegirl said. "You must take Paradise Path to the cross on a hill to see the beautiful view over the river. No other path takes you there."

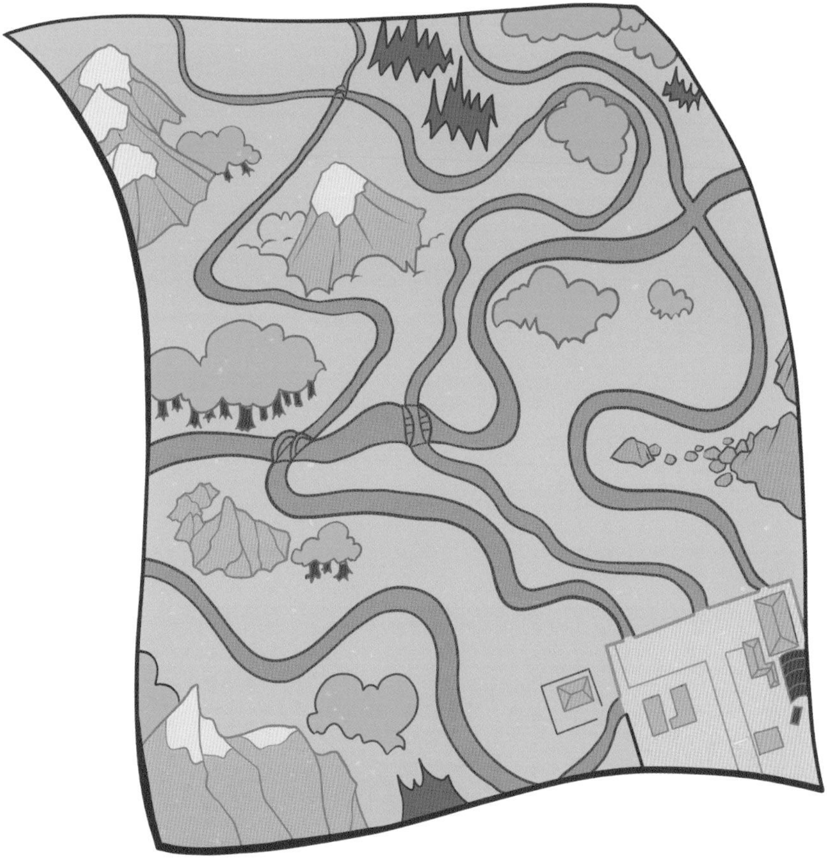

LET'S TALK

If you enjoy hiking or walking trails, what is your favorite place to enjoy God's creation?

Why might Jesus' close friends be confused about what He told them that night?

Why are the cross of Jesus and the empty resurrection tomb so important to us?

Power Word of the Week: FOLLOW

Bibleteam Challenge

Take a walk with a family member and spend time thinking about what Jesus means to you as you talk to Him.

LET'S PRAY TOGETHER

Thank You, Jesus, for making sure I know the only way to heaven. Help me to make sure other people know the way also so we can live forever with You in heaven one day. Amen.

Week 15

Cypher's Guide Lights

Power Bible Verse

Your word is a lamp for my feet and a light on my path. —Psalm 119:105

The Bibleteam walked with Matt and Christopher down the street to their house. The team had rescued the boys from a big battle with evil Luxor Spawndroth.

The sky grew dark as the sun set. The darkness triggered lights to shoot out from each piece of their protective armor. One bright light shone from their helmets, brightening the street ahead. Another light was attached to their shoes of peace, shining on the ground in front of them.

Seeing the lights, Matt and Christopher thought they were cool. Cypher explained they were the new PS119-105 model safety guide lights. The model number helps him remember something important for those who live for Jesus.

"PS119-105 stands for a Bible verse—Psalm 119:105," Cypher explained. "It teaches us that God's Word is a lamp for our feet and a light on our paths. It shows us the way! Whether life is scary or happy, God's Word, the Bible, helps us along each step we take, and it shines like a bright light that guides us to Jesus."

LET'S TALK

Why is it important or helpful that God's Word shows us the way to live and to find life in Jesus?

How can God's Word in the Ten Commandments (Exodus 20:3–17) guide you?

Can you think of a Bible verse or story that has helped or guided you?

Power Word of the Week: GUIDE

Bibleteam Challenge

Try to memorize Psalm 119:105 this week. If you like art, draw a picture of a person walking with lights both directly in front and up ahead, like Psalm 119:105 says.

LET'S PRAY TOGETHER

Heavenly Father, thank You for Your Word that lights my way and leads me to Jesus. Amen.

Week 16

Saving Friend Day

Power Bible Verse

"No one has greater love than this: to lay down his life for his friends." —John 15:13

The night before friend day at school, Mrs. Lesson didn't realize she had left a window open in her classroom. During the night, the Master of Mean wrote mean, mean notes to the students. He folded them into paper airplanes and threw them through the window. The mean notes said, "No one wants to be your friend."

Thankfully, the villain alert woke Bibleman. He helped Cypher grab the long-range, computerized, sucker-upper tube, and they headed to the school. They sucked all of the Master of Mean's notes out the window. Then they made their own fun notes and flew them into the room, like airplanes. Each note said:

Knock, knock.

Who's there?

Dishes.

Dishes who?

Dishes your friend, so open the door!

Then they wrote what Jesus told His disciples: "'I have called you friends, because I have made known to you everything I have heard from my Father'—John 15:15. Smile! Jesus is your best friend! He's knocking on the door of your heart. Invite Jesus in! Happy friend day from the Bibleteam!"

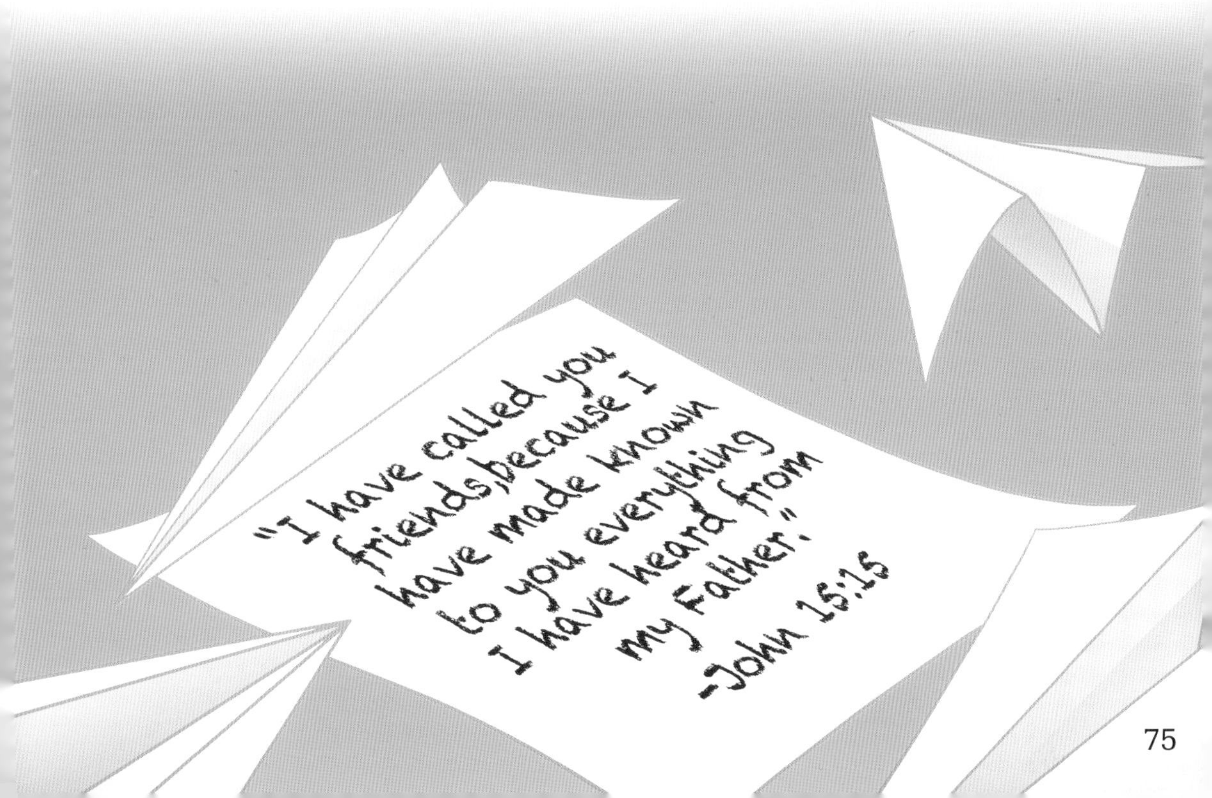
"I have called you
friends, because I
have made known
to you everything
I have heard from
my Father."
-John 15:15

LET'S TALK

Besides Jesus, who is your best friend? What about that person makes him or her a great friend?

Why might other kids say you are a good friend to them?

According to this week's key verse, what is the most amazing thing Jesus did for His friends (us)?

Optional: How does it make you feel that Jesus calls those who follow Him friends?

Power Word of the Week: FRIEND

Bibleteam Challenge

It's easy for friends to thank their friends for being their friend! That may sound confusing, but it's simple. Plan to thank your friends for being your friends this week.

LET'S PRAY TOGETHER

Dear friend, Jesus. It's hard to believe that You call me Your friend. I think I'm no one special, but I realize I must be to You. You gave Your life for me, Your friend—and for the world. Thank You for being my best friend. Amen.

Week 17

Man, Oh Manna!

Power Bible Verse

The Lord had done great things for us; we were joyful. —Psalm 126:3

"I think the Whiner Brothers hung around the wilderness when Moses led God's people to the promised land," Mario told his mom, dad, and sister as he swallowed his soggy breakfast cereal. "God gave them breakfast every day, but they complained because it was the same thing—manna. It fell from the sky while they slept. They'd wake up and complain, 'Man, oh, manna! Again?!'"

"That does sound like the Whiner Brothers' work!" his mother said. "They could have made fun meals out of manna. Meals like scrambled manna, fried manna, or manna sandwiches."

"Instead of being thankful, they grumbled," Dad pointed out. "Maybe they said, *Manna, manna every day. Give us something chickens lay!* Man, oh, manna, God gave them breakfast every day! He was doing great things for them, but they missed His gifts and blessings.

"The Bibleteam would probably tell the Whiner Brothers and us to give thanks and make sure we don't miss the great things God does for us!"

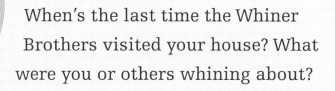

LET'S TALK

When's the last time the Whiner Brothers visited your house? What were you or others whining about?

What are blessings? What are some blessings you received today (or yesterday)?

What are ways you can thank God for all His blessings?

Power Word of the Week: BLESSINGS

Bibleteam Challenge

Try not to whine about anything for the next two days. Tell your family or friends to let you know if you whine. And for the next two days thank God for His blessings at least seven times. You can make that a habit!

LET'S PRAY TOGETHER

Thank You, heavenly Father, for all the great things You do for us! In Jesus' name. Amen.

Week 18

Too Many to Count

Power Bible Verse

God, have mercy on me, a sinner!
—Luke 18:13

Numbers—lots of numbers—covered Cypher's computer screen. His fingers were moving across the keyboard so fast they were out of control!

Melody rushed into the control room. She thought the computer would explode. Cypher looked like he might too! She shouted, "What are you working on? The computer is going crazy!"

"The Ronin of Wrong wanted me to figure out how many times a day we do something wrong—how many times we sin! The numbers won't stop, and that makes Ronin happy!" Cypher told her.

Melody shook her head and said, "We can't keep track. There are too many! James 2:10 says, 'For whoever keeps the entire law, and yet stumbles at one point, is guilty of breaking it all.' We've all broken many, so we're all guilty! Scoot over, Cypher, let me at the keyboard."

Melody typed, "How many of our sins does Jesus forgive?" Three words came up on the screen: *ALL OF THEM!*

"Wow!" Cypher said, surprised. "We don't deserve that! I'm so thankful God had mercy—compassion—on us, even though we don't deserve it!"

LET'S TALK

You can't know or guess how many times you sinned (things you did or didn't do that God wanted or didn't want you to do). But how does sin make you feel?

Why is it sometimes hard to admit you did something wrong and tell someone you're sorry? Is it difficult for you to tell God you're sorry?

How does knowing that Jesus has mercy on you, still loves you, and forgives you make you feel?

Power Word of the Week: MERCY

Bibleteam Challenge

As soon as you realize you have done something you shouldn't have done or didn't do what you should have done this week, stop and tell Jesus or the person you've hurt that you're sorry and ask them for mercy—a caring heart—to forgive you.

LET'S PRAY TOGETHER

God, have mercy on me, a sinner. Thank You, Jesus, for forgiving all the things I've done wrong—all my sins. You forgive and forget my sin. I don't know why You love me so much, but I'm glad You do! Help me learn to love You and others more and more every day. Amen.

Week 19

What Do You Want to Do?

Power Bible Verse

Whatever you do, do it from the heart, as something done for the Lord and not for people. —Colossians 3:23

Marisa decided to make something, anything. But she couldn't decide what. She sat thinking, thinking, thinking. *Build a new city in my computer game? No*, she thought, *that's too hard! Cookies? I'd probably just make a mess. Make a super-cool castle out of blankets and boxes? It might fall apart, and my brother would make fun of me. Draw a super-hero picture? Nah, I'm not a very good artist.*

Marisa's mom walked by and said, "I know what you can make. Your bed!" Marisa rolled her eyes.

She thought she heard the Shadow of Doubt whispering outside her door, "Why do you want to do or make something anyway? No one cares. You might not be good at it."

Suddenly Biblegirl ran into the room, slammed the door on the Shadow of Doubt, and said, "You can do a lot more than you think, Marisa. God gave you talents, but what you do doesn't have to be perfect. Have fun! Learn and try new things! And like Colossians 3:17 says, 'Whatever you do, in word or in deed, do everything in the name of the Lord Jesus, giving thanks to God the Father through him.'" Jesus loves to help you enjoy whatever you do with all He's given you. And don't forget, sometimes you may need to slam the door on the Shadow of Doubt!

LET'S TALK

What talents has God given you? How do you use them?

What talents has God given your family members?

How have you used your talents to serve God or help others?

Power Word of the Week: TALENT

Bibleteam Challenge

Make something! Anything. Big or small. Serious or silly. Ask for help if you need it. Create! Be original! And whatever you create, do the best you can, thanking God that He made it possible.

LET'S PRAY TOGETHER

Thank You, heavenly Father, for giving me the gifts and power to do so many things. I couldn't do them without You. Remind me to do the best I am able with the gifts You have given me. Thank You for creating me as a special child whom You love. Amen.

Week 20

You're Out, Luxor!

Power Bible Verse

I pursue as my goal the prize promised by God's heavenly call in Christ Jesus.—Philippians 3:14

Luxor Spawndroth planned to ruin the T-ball game between T-Time Thunder and Team Victory. He got rid of Thunder's coach so he could manage the team. Luxor planned to make Team Victory's players make mistakes, get distracted, and argue with each other. And he planned to win.

The umpire gathered the teams together before the game. He took off his umpire's mask. It was Bibleman! Luxor and his evil plans would be ruined! Umpire Bibleman told the teams to look at the ball field and remember Psalm 96:12, "Let the fields and everything in them celebrate."

Then Bibleman told both teams to run the bases like it says in Hebrews 12:1–2, with endurance, keeping their eyes on Jesus!

"And don't forget to walk in love like Ephesians 5:2 says, as Christ also loved you and gave Himself for you," Bibleman added.

And when they ran to home plate, Bibleman reminded them to think about how Jesus made it possible for them to reach their goal of heaven. He told them, "Philippians 3:14 says, 'I pursue as my goal the prize promised by God's heavenly call in Christ Jesus.'"

There was one more thing to say. Bibleman looked at Luxor and said, "Luxor, you aren't a real coach, and you don't want the teams to do their best!" With that, Bibleman threw Luxor Spawndroth out of the game so the kids could have fun as ballplayers loved by Jesus!

LET'S TALK

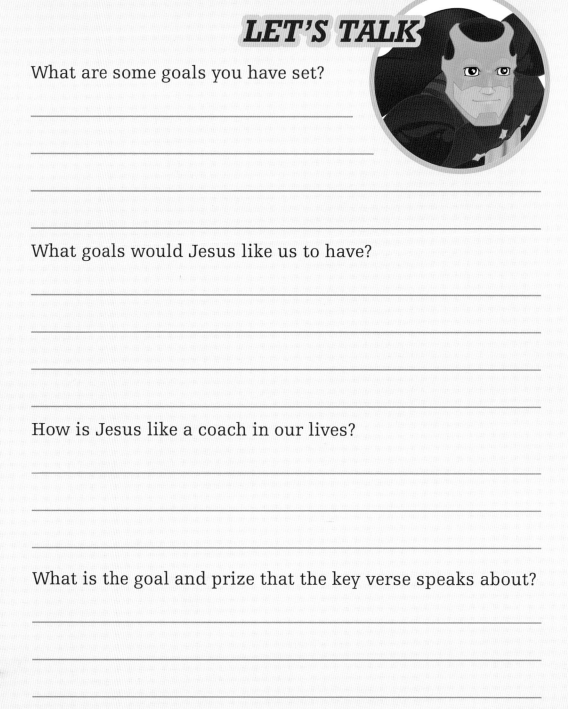

What are some goals you have set?

What goals would Jesus like us to have?

How is Jesus like a coach in our lives?

What is the goal and prize that the key verse speaks about?

Power Word of the Week: GOAL

Bibleteam Challenge

Set two goals for yourself that you can accomplish this week. Choose goals that will make Jesus happy. Think about ways to accomplish your goals, and go do them!

LET'S PRAY TOGETHER

Dear Jesus, our goal of reaching heaven one day is all about You. You have made the goal possible. Living forever with You is the prize. We can't do anything to earn it. Teach us to follow You as You lead us. Amen.

Week 21

Creating a Miracle

Power Bible Verse

**God created man in his own image;
he created him in the image of God;
he created them male and female.
—Genesis 1:27**

Cypher loved creating new devices to help the Bibleteam quickly find villains, defeat them, share God's Word in the Bible with kids, and help kids know, trust, and follow Jesus. It's not easy creating devices like that.

Look around your room right now. What do you think would be the hardest thing in it to make? (I'm waiting for answers.)

Did you choose your body? Did you know you have about 100,000 hairs on your head, 37 trillion living cells, 60,000 miles of blood vessels, and 206 different bones? Your heart beats over 100 times a minute, and you don't even have to tell it to! Wow! God created your body, and He knows every part of it! What an amazing God we have!

King David, in the Bible, was so excited about the body God made him, he wrote, "For it was You who created my inward parts; you knit me together. . . . I will praise you because I have been remarkably and wondrously made. Your works are wondrous, and I know this very well" (Psalm 139:13–14).

LET'S TALK

What do you think is the most amazing miracle about your body God created?

How does learning about God's creation help you want to know more about Him?

What have you created or would like to create some day?

Power Word of the Week: CREATED

Bibleteam Challenge

Ask for help and spend time this week looking up amazing facts about our bodies and all creation. That will help you understand what an awesome God we have. Spend time thanking Him for creating you.

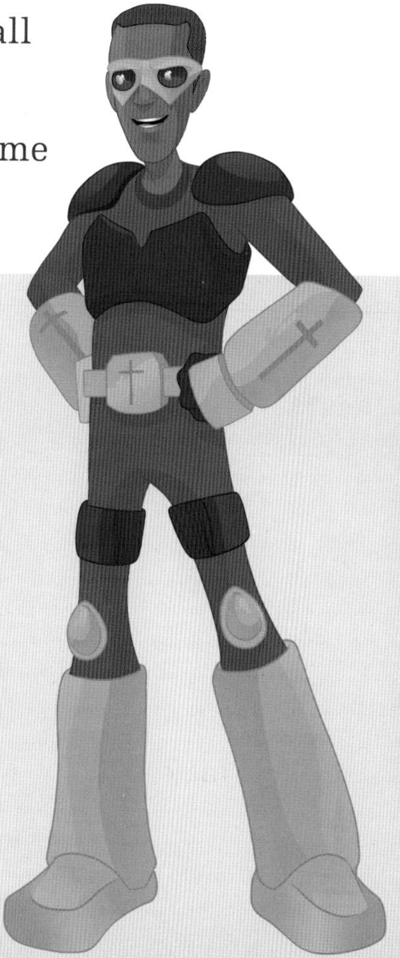

LET'S PRAY TOGETHER

You are amazing, God. You created our bodies and all creation. Wow! You can do all things. You know how much sand is on the beach, and You still care about me. You know everything about me and want to spend time with me forever. Wow! Wow! Wow! Amen.

Week 22

Slacker and Fibbler Team Up

Power Bible Verse

Children, obey your parents in everything, for this pleases the Lord.—Colossians 3:20

Cypher couldn't find Slacker or Fibbler on the radar screen at Bibleteam headquarters. "Are they hiding or just out of range?" he wondered.

Cypher and Melody drove the Biblevan around town, hoping the mobile radar would find them.

Slacker and Fibbler had talked Elijah and his sister, Grace, into ignoring their dad when he had asked them to clean their rooms. Instead, they hid out in the basement family room. Fibbler told the kids to lie about feeling sick, and Slacker gave them headphones so they could watch TV without anyone hearing. Elijah moaned like he was sick, and Grace faked a cough.

Finally, the villains showed up on radar. Cypher and Melody found the kids watching TV while Slacker and Fibbler slept on the floor. Melody yelled to wake them, saying, "Proverbs 6:9—How long will you stay in bed, you slacker?" Then she threw them out of the house.

Cypher used his special remote to change the TV screen to read: "Children, obey your parents in everything, for this pleases the Lord—Colossians 3:20."

The kids told their parents how sorry they were for lying. With their parents' forgiveness, they cleaned their rooms better than ever.

LET'S TALK

Are there chores you could do to help your parents and please Jesus?

What does it mean to respect someone? How does listening to your parents (and others) show them respect?

What's the difference between relaxing and being lazy like Slacker?

Optional: How do your family members respect you? How do you respect them?

Power Word of the Week: RESPECT

Bibleteam Challenge

Ask family members this week what you can do for them. Tell them you don't expect them to do anything in return. You are happy to do it because you respect and care about them.

LET'S PRAY TOGETHER

Dear heavenly Father, so many times this week I have not listened to You or respected You. So many times I did not do what You asked me to. Instead, I did what I wanted. I am so sorry. Forgive me. Help me to change. I know You will. I'm thankful You always love me. You forgive me. I don't know why You do, but You do. Thank You. Thank You. Thank You. I pray in Jesus' name. Amen.

Week 23
The Empress Messes with the King's Kid

Power Bible Verse

Do not grieve, because the joy of the LORD is your strength.
—Nehemiah 8:10

Twins Kate and Tate invited an empress to their "Princess & Pirates" birthday party. They didn't know she was the Empress of Unhappiness! The Empress didn't bring any presents or a smile. Instead, she spotted a "princess" named Joy and went to work. She spilled a drink on Joy's princess dress. She stole her princess crown right off her head! Then she sneezed in Joy's beautiful princess hair. She tried everything to take the joy away from Joy.

Bibleman and Biblegirl were alerted and didn't look happy when they heard what the Empress had done. Bibleman gladly took the Empress away from the party while Biblegirl talked to Joy.

"You know, you won't always feel joyful simply because your name is Joy. We all get sad or upset at times. That's okay! You have the joy of Jesus in you. You're the King's kid!" Biblegirl said. "But that doesn't mean you will always smile and laugh. Not even Jesus did that. He knows what it's like to have sad feelings. He even cried. But even in His sad times, Jesus, our King, had joy in His heart because of His love for us."

Biblegirl continued, "He even died, painfully, on the cross so one day we will be perfectly joyful with Him in heaven forever. Joy, my friend, remember that true joy comes from knowing Jesus and His love no matter how we feel."

LET'S TALK

What gives you a lot of joy? Why?

When we feel sad, what can we remember about Jesus that will help us smile again?

What does it mean if someone calls you a King's kid or a prince or princess of the King?

Optional: What is the joy that Jesus brings you?

Power Word of the Week: JOY

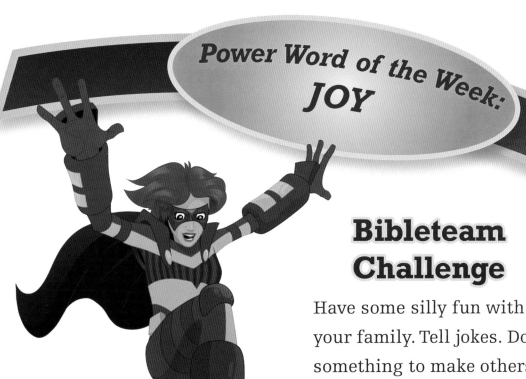

Bibleteam Challenge

Have some silly fun with your family. Tell jokes. Do something to make others laugh. Smile, laugh, and have fun!

LET'S PRAY TOGETHER

Jesus, I won't be happy all the time, but I am happy that even when I'm sad, I have some joy in me because You are in my life. That makes me very happy. Show me ways to bring the joy of Jesus to people and to bring silly joy also. Thank You for creating us to laugh. In Jesus' joyful name I pray. Amen.

Week 24

I Want to See

Power Bible Verse

Sir, we want to see Jesus.
—John 12:21

Joey ran to Jericho Park to hear the Bibleteam talk about Jesus. Joey didn't know much about Jesus. There were so many kids at the park that he couldn't see the Bibleteam. So Joey climbed to the top of the playground set to see.

He listened as Bibleman spoke. "We all do, think, and say things God has told us not to, and we don't do things He wants. That's called sin. We all need someone to save us from our sin and its punishment. So God sent His Son, Jesus, to rescue us! We deserve to be punished for our sins, but Jesus took our punishment for us, in our place! He forgives our sins! He loves us that much!"

Biblegirl reminded the kids, "Jesus will never leave you, forget you, or stop loving you. He will help when you are tempted to do something wrong."

She told a Bible story about Zacchaeus, who wanted to see Jesus and learn more about Him. Then she pointed to the top of the playground equipment and said, "Just like that boy! In the Bible, Zacchaeus climbed a tree to see Jesus. Jesus said He wanted to visit Zacchaeus' house to tell him more about His love." Biblegirl said the same thing to Joey.

So the Bibleteam went to Joey's house. They taught Joey and his parents about Jesus and the Bible. And because of what they heard, Joey's family believed and trusted Jesus!

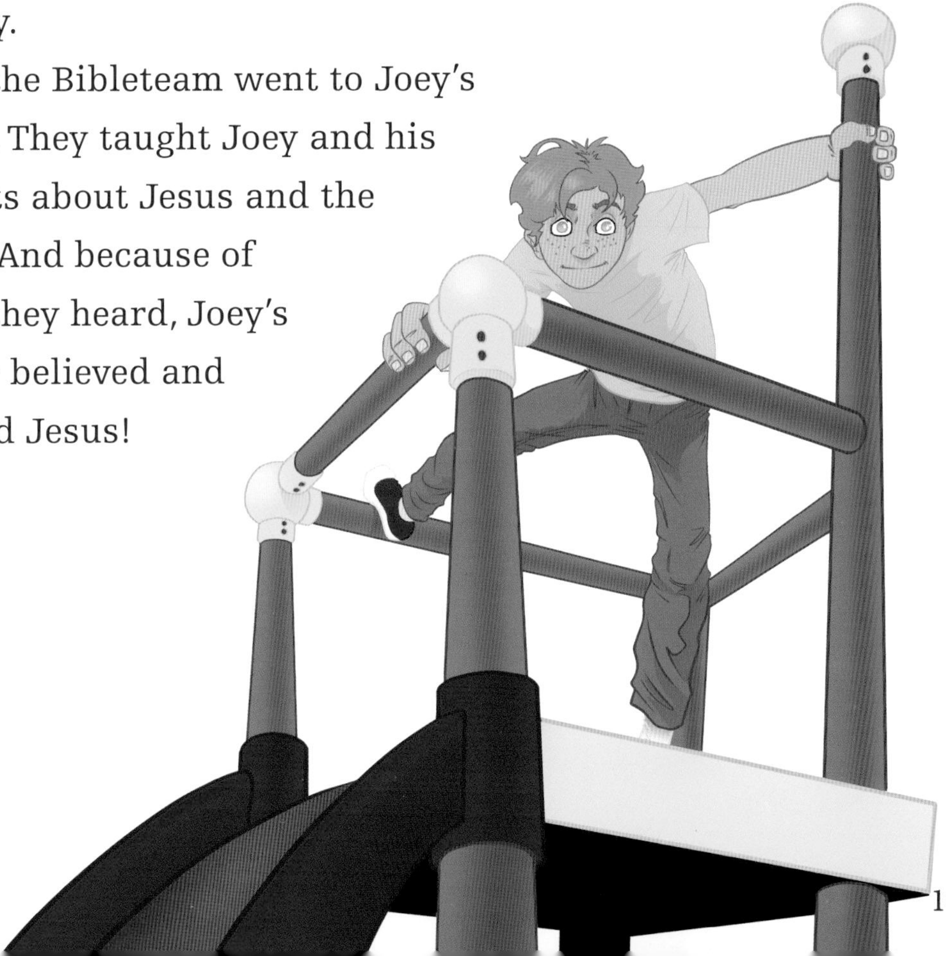

LET'S TALK

When was a time you were too small to see what was going?

If someone visited your house and family, how might they know that Jesus is a part of your lives?

How would you act and what would your family do if Jesus came to visit your house today?

Power Word of the Week: LOOK

Bibleteam Challenge

Read the story of Zacchaeus in Luke 19:1–10 with your family. What did you learn? What does it teach you about your relationship with Jesus? If you know the Zacchaeus song, sing it with your family or act out the story.

LET'S PRAY TOGETHER

Jesus, help me to "see" You when I read Your Word, look at Your awesome creation, talk to people, or worship. Teach me to look for people and places where I can share Your love with others. Thank You for coming to live in my house and life every day. Amen.

Week 25

Waving the Master of Mean Away

Power Bible Verse

The LORD will protect your coming and going both now and forever. —Psalm 121:8

Jackie stood on the beach looking at the ocean waves. The Master of Mean tried to disguise himself to look like a lifeguard. He said, "Are you a scaredy-cat, afraid to go in? The waves won't stop, if that's what you're waiting for! The waves won't wash you away!"

"I won't go in without an adult," Jackie told him, shaking her head. Then she pretended to pull out her shield of faith and hold it in front of her. "You can't hide behind a hat, long Hawaiian shirt, and suntan lotion. I know you're the Master of Mean. I'm thinking about our awesome God who created this ocean. And the non-stop waves remind me that God's love will never end."

Then Jackie pretended to put on the shoes of peace, and she walked down the beach. "When you see footprints like mine, remember Jesus keeps me calm, even when enemies like you come around."

Then Jackie pretended to point the sword of the Spirit at the pretend lifeguard and said, "You don't guard people! You're a fake lifeguard! Psalm 121:8 tells me the LORD will protect my coming and going, both now and forever!" Defeated, the dastardly Master of Mean ran off down the beach, as if her words had kicked sand into his embarrassed face.

LET'S TALK

How has someone protected you, and how have you protected someone?

How did Jackie use the armor of God as protection?

How can knowing Bible verses and stories help protect you?

Power Word of the Week: PROTECTION

Bibleteam Challenge

Have someone help you make a shield, sword, or breastplate out of cardboard or another material to remind you of the protection that comes with the armor of God.

LET'S PRAY TOGETHER

Dear God, You and Your Word have power. Your name has power. And You give me power to fight temptations and God's enemies with Your powerful Word. Protect our home and family. Also protect my faith. I love and trust You, and I don't want anything to hurt that for as long as I live. I pray in the powerful name of Jesus. Amen.

Week 26

The Best of the Boast

Power Bible Verse

Let the one who boasts,
boast in the Lord.
—2 Corinthians 10:17

Randy, Jasmine, Suzi, and Nick couldn't decide what to watch on TV: *Duck-Duck Duo*, *Kangaroo Kickboxers*, *Real Robot Races*, or *Captain Antsinmypants*. What they didn't know was that the Prince of Pride messed with the TV remote. Whenever they tried to change the channel the only show they could watch was *The Next Best Superstar Kid!*

The Prince of Pride told the four friends that the kids on the show were stars. If they acted like those stars, they could tell everyone they were the best—superstar kids! They could brag they were better than their friends. They could get whatever they wanted and do whatever they wanted.

Suddenly Bibleman darted into the room, followed by Cypher. Bibleman told the Prince of Pride that these friends knew God would help them to always do their best. "But," he told the prince, "they don't boast or brag about it. They are humble. They don't think they're better than anyone else. But they do tell others about the great ways of Jesus! They brag about Jesus, their best friend. The best of the best."

With that, Bibleman sent the Prince of Pride out the door along with a Bible verse from Psalm 44:8: "We boast in God all day long; we will praise your name forever." Cypher fixed the remote, and the kids laughed when they saw the name of the TV show he turned on: *The Adventures of Humblebee, the Bumblebee*.

LET'S TALK

What does *humble* mean?

Name some people who seem very humble.

How can we do our best at something and be very good but still stay humble? Who should get the praise for the good or great things we do?

Optional: Name some Bible characters who were humble.

Power Word of the Week: HUMBLE

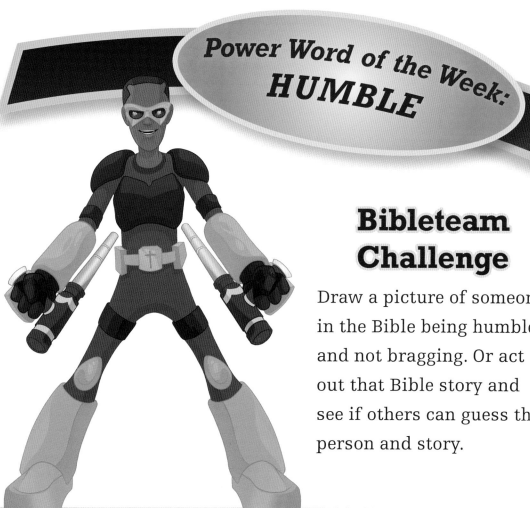

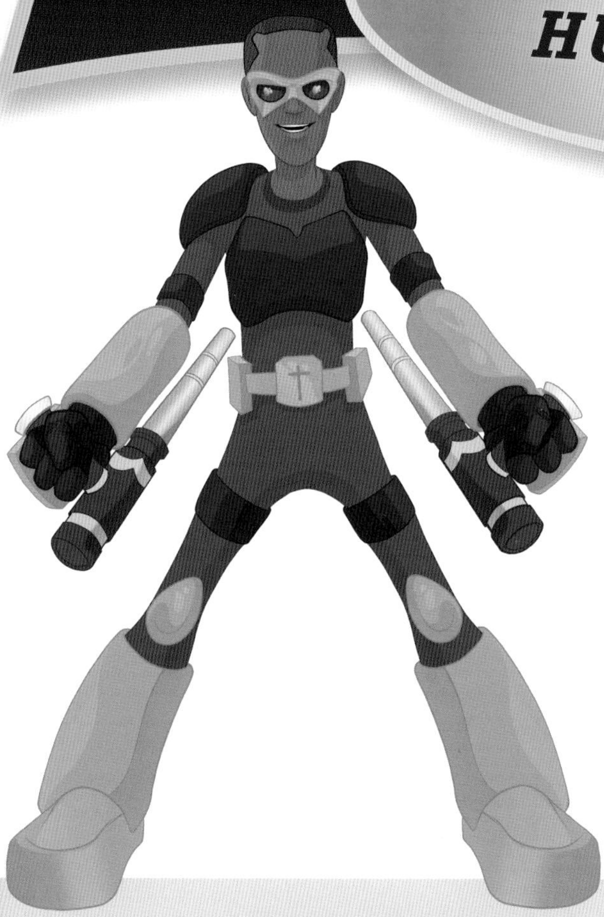

Bibleteam Challenge

Draw a picture of someone in the Bible being humble and not bragging. Or act out that Bible story and see if others can guess the person and story.

LET'S PRAY TOGETHER

Jesus, may all my boasting and bragging be about how great You are in every way, every day. May I use the talents You have given me to praise Your name and not my own. I humbly pray in Your great name. Amen.

Week 27 Finding Courage without a Shadow of Doubt

Power Bible Verse

The LORD is the one who will go before you. He will be with you; he will not leave you or abandon you. Do not be afraid or discouraged.
—Deuteronomy 31:8

Kwan's mom made his favorite mint milkshake after lunch. What he didn't know was that the sneaky Shadow of Doubt took the real mint out of the kitchen and replaced it with discourage-mints.

After his snack Kwan didn't feel well. He also didn't have courage to ask his new neighbor, Sam, to go to kids' church with him. Kwan couldn't figure out why he was discouraged or why he thought Sam wouldn't want to go. He'd hoped to have the courage to share Jesus with Sam.

Kwan's dad noticed Kwan wasn't acting like he normally did, so they talked about it. Kwan and his dad knew asking Sam to kids' church was the right thing to do.

Jesus' friends got courage by trusting Him and His promises! Kwan and his dad decided that before he went to Sam's house they would go to Jesus in prayer. Jesus would gladly give Kwan courage!

That prayer shed light on the Shadow of Doubt, who took his discourage-mints and bolted, staying far away from the neighborhood. Thankfully, Jesus stayed close when Sam went with Kwan to kids' church that week!

LET'S TALK

What does the word *discourage* mean?

When have you wanted to ask someone to go to church, Sunday school, VBS, or something similar, but didn't? Share about that experience.

How do people get courage just knowing Jesus is with them?

Power Word of the Week: COURAGE

Bibleteam Challenge

Think of a person who doesn't usually go to church. Pray that the Holy Spirit will give you the courage to ask him or her to go with you. Talk to your parents about it. Then invite them to go! It's really not hard!

LET'S PRAY TOGETHER

Holy Spirit, help me think of people who don't know Jesus that I could invite to go to our church with us. I feel like I need courage, but then I also know I'm just asking them to meet You—and that's the best invitation ever! Use me to bring more and more people to know You. I pray in Jesus' name. Amen.

Week 28

A Brush with the Fibbler

Power Bible Verse

Keep falsehood and deceitful words far from me.
—Proverbs 30:8

Ben!" his mom called out. "Did you brush your teeth? It's time for bed."

"Um, Aah emm, gurgle, gurgle. Whoettt nowwh," Ben mumbled loudly from the bathroom, pretending he was brushing his teeth. "All done!"

A few minutes later, his mom came into his room. She didn't look happy. "Ben, it doesn't look like you brushed your teeth. Your toothbrush wasn't even wet. Are you telling me the truth?"

"I am! My toothbrush dries fast." Ben lied. His mom didn't say anything, but instead game him "the look." "Okay, you're right, Mom. I'm sorry. I didn't brush them. Will you forgive me?"

"I forgive you, Ben. Thank you for telling the truth and asking for forgiveness," his mom said, giving him a hug. "It sounds like the Fibbler might have shown up, but Bibleman chased him off. He might have reminded us that the Bible says in Colossians 3:9, 'Do not lie to one another.' The truth is it's time for bed. But first, brush your teeth. This time use the toothbrush!"

"Thanks for forgiving me, Mom!" Ben said. "And thank You, Jesus, for forgiving me too!"

LET'S TALK

If you have ever lied, how did you feel afterward?

When you were forgiven, how did you feel afterward?

How do people try to lie to God? Is it possible to do that?

Optional: Who told the first lie in the Bible? (Hint: Genesis 3:1–4)

Power Word of the Week: TRUTH

Bibleteam Challenge

The next time you are tempted to lie remember the Fibbler and run him off. And then, when you brush your teeth tonight (or in the morning) with a parent around, say, "I love you, and that's the tooth, I mean truth."

LET'S PRAY TOGETHER

Jesus, You cannot and do not lie. Help me to tell the truth at all times. I'm so glad I know the truth that You love me, forgive me, and want to be with me forever! In Your perfect name I pray. Amen.

Week 29

Crushing Crusher with God's Word

Power Bible Verse

If possible, as far as it depends on you, live at peace with everyone. —Romans 12:18

Owen and Austin were kicking a soccer ball around when some older kids stomped into the yard. They made fun of Owen and Austin, pushed them, and called them names. Crusher had convinced the bullies to start a neighborhood battle with the younger kids. He showed them how to fight like the bots in their video games.

The Bibleteam was alerted. They arrived quickly and surrounded Crusher. Crusher roared and raised his big fists to fight.

The Bibleteam's shields of faith were activated, protecting them when Crusher threw a punch. Armed with the sword of the Spirit, Bibleman fearlessly warned Crusher that they fight evil with God's Word. Colossians 3:8 tells us to put away anger, meanness, and bad language. Jesus can replace your anger with His peace. Crusher, though, didn't want anything to do with peace, and he dashed away.

Then the Bibleteam reminded the boys, "When you ask the Holy Spirit to help you throw out unkindness and anger and forgive instead, you'll have peace and joy."

Soon all the kids were playing soccer together, laughing, and having fun.

LET'S TALK

Have you ever been bullied? Have you ever been the bully? What were your feelings at that time?

How would you describe what peace is or feels like?

Is peace that Jesus gives different from your last answer? How is or isn't it?

Optional: How do you usually deal with kids who are mean to you? What might be the best way?

Power Word of the Week: PEACE

Bibleteam Challenge

This is a difficult challenge. Jesus asks that we pray for our enemies. It's hard to stay mad at someone as we pray for them. Pray for help and forgiveness.

LET'S PRAY TOGETHER

Heavenly Father, I know every day won't be peaceful. I'm glad You share Your peace that is different from the ways I try to find it. I pray that You would protect me from any enemies or bullies. But also make them nicer. I want to show them the love of Jesus. Help me forgive them as You have forgiven me. And if I have been mean to someone, give me courage to go to them and ask forgiveness. Thank You. Amen.

Week 30
Jesus and Four-Legged Friend Defeat Loneliness

Power Bible Verse

A friend loves at all times.
—Proverbs 17:17

The Empress of Unhappiness slipped lonely thoughts into Grayson's mind. He lounged on the sofa with Sadie, his dog, curled up next to him. Grayson hadn't made friends at his new school or in the neighborhood. His mom and dad had important jobs that kept them busy. His sitter liked to sit and play games on her phone. Sadie looked at him and seemed to smile as he pet her.

Cypher received a sad sounding villain alert at Bibleteam headquarters. He immediately sent a drone to Grayson's house. He programmed the drone to play Christian worship music in the house to praise Jesus and encourage Grayson. Cypher knew the Empress of Unhappiness couldn't stand that music and would leave in a hurry.

Then Cypher sent Grayson a voice-message through the drone reminding him that his perfect friend, Jesus, will always love and will never leave him. Cypher also shared that God blessed him with a loving, four-legged friend.

Cypher was right! Sadie was always happy to see him, played with him whenever he wanted, and always made him feel loved. He thanked Jesus for His perfect love and for the love of his four-legged friend, Sadie.

LET'S TALK

When have you felt like Grayson—alone and unloved? What made you feel better?

How can pets be our friends? How might they help us?

If you have a pet, have you thanked God for him or her? If you don't, do you have a stuffed animal, toy, or something else that helps you feel loved?

Power Word of the Week: FRIENDS

Bibleteam Challenge

If you have a pet, do something special for it, if you're able to. Do something special for one of your human friends, too, so they know how much you care.

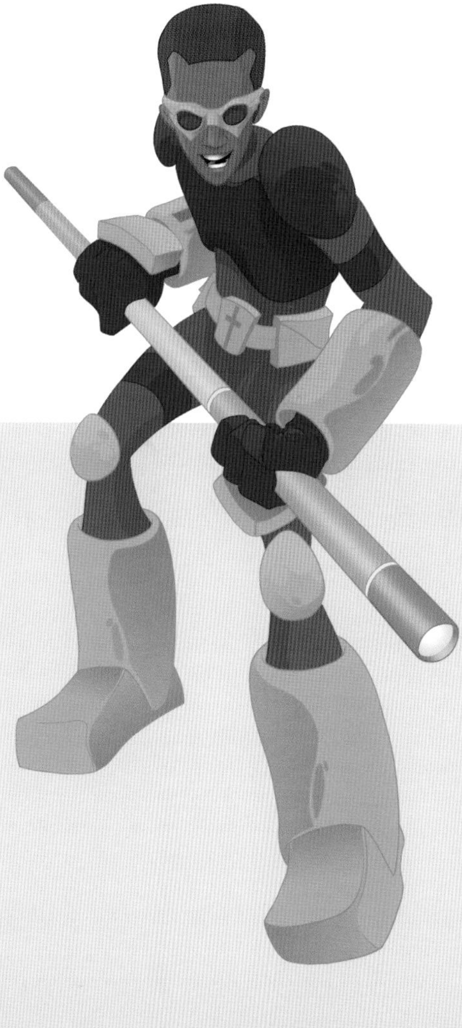

LET'S PRAY TOGETHER

Thank You for being my friend, Jesus. You never leave me. You never stop loving me. I'm also thankful for my people and animal friends. They are all special gifts from You. Amen.

Week 31

The Power of Sharing

Power Bible Verse

Don't neglect to do what is good and to share.
—Hebrews 13:16

The Grand Duchess of Greed told Jason not to share his superhero toys with his school friends. Thankfully, Bibleman appeared and reminded Jason and the class what happened when a boy shared his lunch with Jesus. "Jesus loved teaching people what trusting God means," Bibleman began. "He loved to teach about God's forgiveness and love and about the importance of sharing His love and good news with others.

"One day when Jesus was teaching it got to be late, and His friends—five thousand of them—were getting hungry. Close friends of Jesus wanted to send the people home so they could get something to eat. But Jesus wanted them to see His power and goodness. They found a boy in the crowd with five loaves of bread and two fish. But could so little feed so many?

"The boy gave them to Jesus. He prayed to His Father in heaven, thanking Him for the food. Then Jesus and His friends shared the fish and bread. Everyone had plenty of food to eat. There were even leftovers! What a miracle!"

We never know what Jesus will do when we share what we have with Him and others!

LET'S TALK

Name some times when it's fun and easy to share. Name some times when it is harder to share.

How might you have acted if you were in that crowd when Jesus fed all those people?

If you had been there, would you tell others about Jesus? A couple or a lot?

Power Word of the Week: SHARE

Bibleteam Challenge

Bake or cook something with the help of an adult this week. Look at what you made and then try to imagine how much more you'd need to feed over five thousand people!

LET'S PRAY TOGETHER

You are amazing, Jesus! Your miracles show that You are God. Thank You for the miracles all around me. Help me to be amazed at all You do and always praise You. Amen.

Week 32

On Our Side, by Our Side

Power Bible Verse

"Haven't I commanded you: be strong and courageous? Do not be afraid or discouraged, for the LORD your God is with you wherever you go."
—Joshua 1:9

The Bibleteam visited Vacation Bible School. The first day of VBS, a boy asked the team if fighting villains was scary work.

Bibleman told the kids, "Our strength isn't enough. God's power and strength overcome villains through Jesus! We use God's Word, the Bible. Through it, God helps people know and trust Jesus. Knowing Jesus is on our side and by our side, fighting for us and through us, gives us confidence!" The kids clapped, whooped, and cheered!

Bibleman told the kids what God told His people in Deuteronomy 20:3–4: "Today you are about to engage in battle with your enemies. Do not be cowardly. Do not be afraid, alarmed, or terrified because of them. For the LORD your God is the one who goes with you to fight for you against your enemies to give you victory."

Biblegirl and the kids chanted over and over, "God is by our side! There is no need for fear! Jesus fights for us! Let's shout His victory cheer!"

8 This book of instruction must not depart from your mouth; you are to meditate on it day and night so that you may carefully observe everything written in it. For then you will prosper and succeed in whatever you do.
9 Haven't I commanded you: be strong and courageous? Do not be afraid or discouraged, for the LORD your God is with you wherever you go."
10 Then Joshua commanded the officers of the people: 11 "Go through the camp and tell the people, 'Get provisions ready for yourselves, for within three days you will be crossing the Jordan to go in and take possession of the land the LORD your God is giving you to inherit.'"

LET'S TALK

If you were Bibleman and someone asked you if fighting villains was scary work, what would you say?

Read this week's key verse again. How does it make you feel?

When do you feel strong? When do you feel weak?

Power Word of the Week: STRONG

Bibleteam Challenge

Say Biblegirl's victory cheer three times. That might help you remember it so you can shout it in your head when you're feeling weak, lonely, or tempted.

LET'S PRAY TOGETHER

Jesus, thank You for Your promise to stay with me. You fight for me. You get rid of fear. We cheer and praise You for the victories You've won for us. The most important victory is when You defeated Satan and sin on the cross and rose on Easter morning. Thank You! Praise God! Amen.

Week 33

Wearing the Armor of God

Power Bible Verse

Put on the full armor of God so that you can stand against the schemes of the devil.—Ephesians 6:11

On the second day of Vacation Bible School, Bibleman reminded the kids about the armor he wears to defeat villains and lead kids to Jesus Christ. The Bible, in Ephesians 6:13–17, calls it the armor of God.

- **Helmet of Salvation** (v. 17)—A big hit to the head would be a bad injury. It could kill someone. Trusting in Jesus as our Savior is like a helmet. It cannot be broken.
- **Breastplate of Righteousness** (v. 14)—This protects your heart and lungs. Being righteous means to live a sinless life. But we can't do that! So Jesus covers and protects us with His perfect righteousness. We're armed with Jesus Himself!

- **Belt of Truth** (v. 14)—This helps us fight God's enemies without falling. In Bible times, people recognized leaders by the belt they wore. And it would hold the sword of God's truth.
- **Shield of Faith** (v. 16)—The shield protects us from Satan's lies and temptations.
- **Sword of the Spirit** (v. 17)—When Jesus was tempted, He attacked the devil with God's Word. The Holy Spirit works His power through God's Word.
- **Shoes of Peace** (v. 15)—They protect us and keep us from slipping. We can stand strong on God's promises of love, forgiveness, and strength.

"This armor is for each of us to wear," Bibleman told the kids.

The kids took turns pretending to put on every piece of the armor of God. Then they posed like Bibleman—strong and unafraid.

LET'S TALK

Do you think one piece of the armor is more important than the others?

What does the Sword of the Spirit stand for? How does Bibleman use it to defeat enemies?

How does it feel to be covered in the protection, perfection, and strength of Jesus?

Power Word of the Week: ARMOR

Bibleteam Challenge

Draw a picture of the pieces of armor. This week, pretend you are putting each piece on while you get dressed. See if that changes the way you think, act, and rely on Jesus.

LET'S PRAY TOGETHER

Jesus, keep the devil and enemies far away from me. Thank You for reminding me how You cover and protect me every day with Your armor. In Your strong name I pray. Amen.

Week 34

No More Stinkin' Thinkin'

Power Bible Verse

Finally, brothers and sisters, whatever is true, whatever is honorable, whatever is just, whatever is pure, whatever is lovely, whatever is commendable—if there is any moral excellence and if there is anything praiseworthy—dwell on these things.—Philippians 4:8

The Bibleteam visited Vacation Bible School again. On the third day of VBS, Biblegirl shared about the day God's Word overpowered the Empress of Unhappiness.

"While Mrs. Simpson's first-grade class was at recess, the Empress of Unhappiness filled their classroom air with Stinkin' Thinkin'! After recess, the kids started thinking sad thoughts, mean thoughts, feeling-sorry-for-themselves thoughts."

Biblegirl continued, "The Bibleman headquarters alerted me about the threatening activity. Cypher knew fighting unhappiness was right down my alley. Thankfully the school was also right down the alley, so I arrived quickly. I heard the Empress laughing, thinking about the mess she had made. She saw me and ran. But she heard me say I would clear the classroom air with God's Word, turning the Stinkin' Thinkin' into Joyful Jesus Thinkin'!"

"And that's what happened," Biblegirl explained. "I told the kids about the Bible's wise reminder in Philippians 4:8. The Holy Spirit helped them think about what is kind and helpful, good and pleasing to God, and things that give praise to Jesus, who loves them!"

LET'S TALK

What thoughts could be called Stinkin' Thinkin'?

What thoughts could be called Joyful Jesus Thinkin'?

What did you spend a lot of time thinking about today?

Power Word of the Week: THINK

Bibleteam Challenge

Make a list of the things God would have us think about that are found in the key verse. With the help of an adult, give examples of those thoughts.

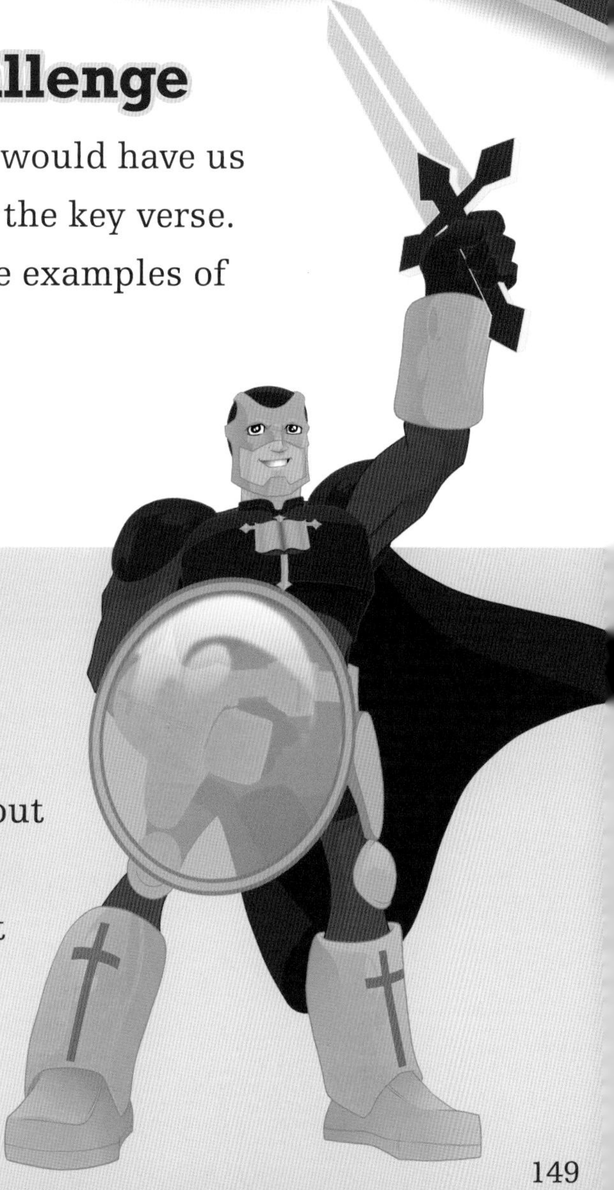

LET'S PRAY TOGETHER

Dear Jesus, help me think about You more every day because I want to learn to think and act like You. I need Your help. What do You think about that, Jesus? Amen.

Week 35

Better as a Team

Power Bible Verse

Be diligent to present yourself to God as one approved, a worker who doesn't need to be ashamed, correctly teaching the word of truth. —2 Timothy 2:15

The fourth day the Bibleteam visited Vacation Bible School, Cypher and Melody taught the children about teamwork. Working together is very important!

"Everyone on the Bibleteam is different," Cypher explained. "I'm better with computers and devices than Biblegirl. She's faster, stronger, and a better singer!" he said with a smile. "Melody loves helping us work together with new ideas. And she's great at gymnastics. Watch out, here she comes!"

Melody ran onto the stage and did a front-aerial walk-over gymnastic move. The kids cheered and clapped.

"Bibleman," Melody told the kids, "was blessed as a great leader who is smart and strong. We all love Jesus, the Bible, and praying together. And we love telling others about Jesus. He's the real hero who rescued us all from sin. We do our best and work together as a team to defeat villains with God's Word. Together we're stronger and smarter, and we do God's work better as a team."

The Bibleteam stood together as Bibleman prayed for the VBS kids and gave thanks to Jesus, the world's true hero. And all the kids shouted, "Amen!"

LET'S TALK

What activities do you do with someone else?

Why is working together important?

How did Jesus work with people when He lived on earth?

Optional: What's something you can't do very well without others?

Power Word of the Week: TEAMWORK

Bibleteam Challenge

Help a family member or friend do a chore.

LET'S PRAY TOGETHER

Jesus, thank You for being with me all day. You make my days easier, since we are a team. Forgive me when I don't let You help me. Help me to be a good teammate and helper, doing the best I can with Your help. You are my best friend! Amen.

Week 36

The Bibleman Song

Power Bible Verse

Take up the full armor of God, so that you may be able to resist in the evil day, and having prepared everything, to take your stand.—Ephesians 6:13

The Bibleteam visited on the fifth day of Vacation Bible School. The team knew the kids loved to sing, so on the last day of VBS they taught everyone the official Bibleman theme song! One child made up hand and body motions for everyone to use as they sang!

Bibleman! Bibleman!

Fighting for the way, he's the Bibleman.

Bibleman! Fighting the good fight,

Taking the shield of faith and the belt of truth, Bibleman is on the move.

The sword of the Spirit is the Word of God. There's nothing it can't do.

Bibleman! Bibleman! Fighting the good fight,

Wearing the breastplate of righteousness and the helmet of salvation.

Biblegirl, Cypher, and Melody—fighting for the way.

We stand together in the sight of God.

We stand together to do what's right.

Bibleman! Bibleman!

Fighting for God's truth and way!

"It's fun to make hand motions when we sing," Bibleman said. "Jesus made the most important hand motions for us. He stretched out His hands on the cross because He loves us. He died and rose from the dead, forgiving sins and sharing the gift of heaven. We love and forgive because Jesus first loved and forgave us. Sing a song of thanks to Jesus! Clap your hands to praise Him!"

LET'S TALK

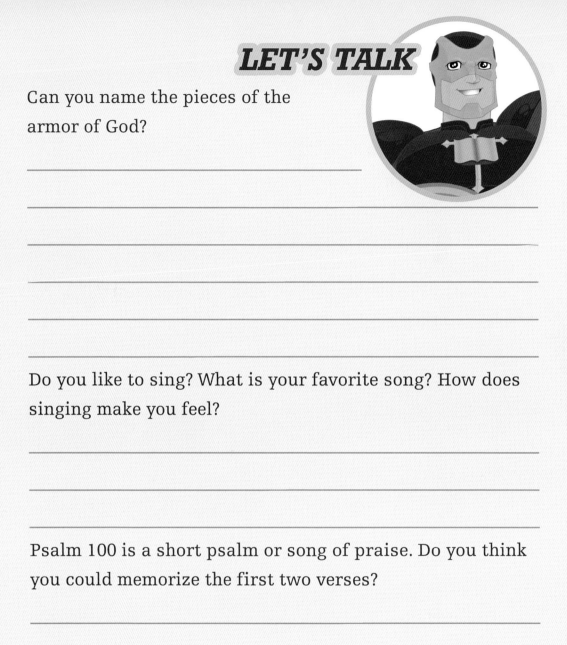

Can you name the pieces of the armor of God?

Do you like to sing? What is your favorite song? How does singing make you feel?

Psalm 100 is a short psalm or song of praise. Do you think you could memorize the first two verses?

Power Word of the Week: *SING*

Bibleteam Challenge

Even if you don't know the music to the Bibleman song, create hand and body motions that go with the words. Have fun acting them out as an adult reads (or sings) the words.

LET'S PRAY TOGETHER

Dear Jesus, thank You for using the Bibleteam to teach me about strength, using the armor of God, and Your love. And thank You for the gift of songs and music to praise You and help me trust in You in all things. Amen.

Week 37

Bibleman's New GPS

Power Bible Verse

So faith comes from what is heard, and what is heard comes through the message about Christ.
—Romans 10:17

Driving down Romans Road, Bibleman thanked Melody for putting the new GPS monitor on the back of his shield of faith. It gave fast directions to kids needing help. But the screen also showed a different kind of GPS: **G**od's **P**lan of **S**alvation. That's the plan God used to rescue the world from sin and other enemies. It leads kids to Jesus Christ using these Bible verses:

- **Romans 3:23**—For all have sinned and fall short of the glory of God. (*We all disappoint God and hurt others.*)
- **Romans 5:8**—But God proves his own love for us in that while we were still sinners, Christ died for us. (*Jesus took our punishment and died for us.*)

- **Romans 6:23**—For the wages of sin is death, but the gift of God is eternal life in Christ Jesus our Lord. (*Because Jesus died for us, we will live forever with God.*)
- **Romans 10:9**—If you confess with your mouth, "Jesus is Lord," and believe in your heart that God raised him from the dead, you will be saved. (*Believe in Jesus and tell others!*)
- **Romans 10:13**—For everyone who calls on the name of the Lord will be saved.

Becoming a Christian is as simple as believing these Bible verses and receiving the free gifts of forgiveness and unending life Jesus wants to give you.

LET'S TALK

What are some things you believe about Jesus?

What are some words or ideas you may not understand in the verses above?

What is faith?

Power Word of the Week: *FAITH*

Bibleteam Challenge

Share this devotion with everyone in your house. Talk about what it means for them and ask if they believe the words.

LET'S PRAY TOGETHER

Jesus, I believe. I believe You are my Savior—Rescuer from my mess of sin. I believe You died and rose from the dead for me. I believe You are the only way to heaven. I believe You will always love me and never leave me. Thank You, Holy Spirit, for making it possible for me to believe those true words. In Jesus' name. Amen.

Week 38

I Don't Understand. Do You?

Power Bible Verse

Then [Jesus] opened their minds to understand the Scriptures. —Luke 24:45

Biblegirl visited with Sophia and her family at the park. Sophia told Biblegirl she loved family devotions and going to kids' church. "But," she admitted, "sometimes the Bible is hard to understand." Biblegirl agreed! And so did Sophia's brother and parents.

So Biblegirl told them this story from Acts 8:26–40. "While traveling, a man read from the Old Testament book of Isaiah. Philip, a close friend of Jesus, asked the man, 'Do you understand what you are reading?' The man said he needed someone to explain it to him. So Philip took the time to help him and to explain God's Word."

"So we should ask questions when we don't understand something," Sophia asked, "just like we do with other books and stories?"

"You're right," her mom added. "But we know the Bible is not like any other book. It's God's Word. It's the true story of God's love for the people He created. The Bible is about Jesus and how He lives so that we can have a forgiven and unending life with Him from the first pages to the last."

LET'S TALK

What Bible ideas are hard for you to understand?

Who will you ask to help you?

Ask others in your home what Bible ideas are hard for them to understand. Try to find someone to help them understand.

Power Word of the Week: UNDERSTAND

Bibleteam Challenge

Memorize the names of the first five books of the Old Testament and the first four books of the New Testament this week.

LET'S PRAY TOGETHER

Dear God—Father, Son, and Holy Spirit—thank You for Your Word, the Bible. Help me to learn more about it because then I will know more about You. Please put people in my life who can help me understand the Bible better. Thank You for those who help me now. Grow my faith. I pray in Jesus' name. Amen.

Week 39
Luxor Gives Parents a Bad Rap

Power Bible Verse

Honor your father and mother.
—Ephesians 6:2

Luxor Spawndroth didn't want kids to listen to their parents. The people at the town talent show found that out. In the middle of the show, Luxor ran onstage, grabbed the microphone and started rapping!

Your parents say "Obey." You say, "No way!"
Your parents say, "Please stay." You go astray!
Your parents say, "Let's pray." You say, "Let's play!"

"Quick," said Melody, "close the stage curtains!" Melody told the crowd how sorry she was they had to hear that. She reassured them that Luxor's way is not God's way and that Bibleman was taking care of Luxor.

Suddenly, Biblegirl ran on stage and rapped,

Your parents say, "Obey." You gladly say, "Okay!"

Your parents say, "Please stay." You gladly say, "Okay!"

Your parents say, "Let's pray." You gladly say, "Okay!"

Cypher put a sticker on Luxor's back, and as Bibleman walked Luxor out of the building, everyone clapped because the sticker said, "Children, obey your parents in the Lord, because this is right—Ephesians 6:1."

LET'S TALK

Why do we obey our parents?

Why are parents so smart?

Is there ever a time when you would not listen to your parents?

Optional: Imagine you're a parent (many, many years from now). What do you think you'll do when your children don't listen and obey?

Bibleteam Challenge

Give your parents or guardians a hug, tell them you love them, and thank them every day this week. Who knows, maybe you'll do it every day of the year!

LET'S PRAY TOGETHER

Jesus, forgive me when I don't listen to my parents—or You. Help me gladly obey their words spoken in love. Thank You for all the adults in my life who love me and take care of me. I know they are gifts from You. I love You, Jesus. Amen.

Week 40

Olivia's Psalm

Power Bible Verse

"I am the good shepherd. I know my own, and my own know me."
—John 10:14

Olivia remembered when Bibleman fought Dr. Fear and told kids about Psalm 23. So she asked her mom to help her write her own psalm (which is a prayer or song).

Oliva's Psalm 23
The Lord is my shepherd. He's all I need!
He lets me have fun in the green grass;
He takes me to quiet and peaceful places.
He gives me a new kind of life, through Jesus;
And leads me in the right direction, to Jesus.
Even when I go through scary or sad times,
I am not afraid, for You are with me;
You know how to make me feel safe.

Even when kids are mean or

I face enemies like Dr. Fear,

You will take care of me and love me.

Your goodness and never-ending love will always stay with me!

Yes, I will be with You forever!

Olivia and her mom planned to write more psalms another day.

LET'S TALK

What lines or thoughts in Olivia's psalm do you like the best? Why?

____

____

____

What does this week's key verse mean to you?

____

____

____

Read Psalm 23 in the Bible and share your thoughts.

____

____

____

Optional: What are some favorite psalms of someone you live with, if any?

____

____

____

Power Word of the Week: PSALM

Bibleteam Challenge

Have someone help you write your own psalm.

LET'S PRAY TOGETHER

You are my shepherd and that is all I need! Thank You for caring for me, leading me, and protecting me. I love knowing I will be with You forever. I pray in Jesus' name. Amen.

Week 41

The Mayor Learns the Truth

Power Bible Verse

It is impossible for God to lie.
—Hebrews 6:18

The Mayor of Maybe almost got Liam to believe God could lie. Almost! Liam's friend lied to his mom about eating the last cupcake. Becky's dad didn't come to her dance class even though he promised. And Liam lied when he told his sister their dog spilled juice on her book. So Liam wondered if God lied.

Thankfully, Bibleman caught the Mayor of Maybe before he confused Liam about God's truth. He drew his sword and said, "It is impossible for God to lie—Hebrews 6:18!" Those words turned the Mayor's lies to dust and chased them down the road. "When God makes a promise, you know it's true," Bibleman told Liam.

You should know these and all promises of God are true:

- For I will forgive their wrongdoing, and I will never again remember their sins.—Hebrews 8:12
- "Call to me and I will answer you."—Jeremiah 33:3
- "And remember, I am with you always."—Matthew 28:20
- "God . . . gave his one and only Son, so that everyone who believes in him will not perish but have eternal life."—John 3:16

LET'S TALK

What are some promises you didn't keep or lies you told that you are sorry for telling?

How do lies hurt people?

What is your favorite promise God has given?

Optional: How have God's promises changed your life?

Power Word of the Week: PROMISES

Bibleteam Challenge

Write one or more of God's promises from the Bible to keep with you or in your room.

LET'S PRAY TOGETHER

Your promises help me so much. I know you will always tell me the truth. Thank You, Jesus, for all Your promises and love. Amen.

Week 42 The Invisible Dr. Fear Disappears Again

Power Bible Verse

The battle is the LORD's.

—1 Samuel 17:47

Davey pretended to fish off the side of his tree house. He couldn't see Dr. Fear in his invisible mode, but Davey had a feeling he was around, planting seeds of fear. So he said, "I know you're there, Dr. Fear. I'm not afraid. I think you're afraid to show yourself! Bibleman taught me something that keeps me from being afraid. He reminded me that I'm named after David in the Bible. David had a lot to be afraid of, but he trusted God. As a shepherd, David rescued lambs from lions and bears. He defeated and killed his giant enemy, Goliath. King Saul even tried to kill David, but he escaped. David also led armies into battle, and he did much more. "

"When I'm afraid I remember David, Bible verses, Bibleman, and especially Jesus, the bravest and best of them all," Davey added. "I like what David wrote in Psalm 27:1, 'The LORD is my light and my salvation—whom should I fear?'"

Davey never heard from Dr. Fear again. He must have disappeared. But who knows, since he was invisible!

LET'S TALK

When we become afraid, what is the best thing to remember?

Do you think Jesus was ever afraid? When?

At times we are afraid because we aren't trusting God. But are there times when being afraid of something is good—to keep us safe?

Optional: Besides Jesus, who helps you when you feel afraid?

Power Word of the Week: FEARLESS

Bibleteam Challenge

Memorize this week's key verse. Draw a picture of one of the ways David was fearless.

LET'S PRAY TOGETHER

Fearless God, help me to trust You and pray to You when I am afraid. Thank You for people, pets, and things that help me feel less afraid. Help me to be more like David and Jesus every day. I love and trust You. Amen.

Week 43

Bibleman and His Beautiful Feet

Power Bible Verse

How beautiful on the mountains are the feet of the herald, who proclaims peace, who brings news of good things, who proclaims salvation, who says to Zion, "Your God reigns!"

—Isaiah 52:7

The Bibleteam told kids at Resurrection Church that people who lived long ago when the Bible was written didn't have phones, TVs, or computers to find out what was going on. The kids couldn't imagine living like that!

Bibleman told them that when God's people went to battle against enemies, their families at home waited excitedly to get news. Messengers would run from the battlefield with news. The people watched and waited! As soon as they saw the messenger in the distance, they could tell if he had good news or bad. If his feet moved fast and he looked excited, the enemy had been defeated! They told everyone the good news of victory and peace!

Isaiah 52:7 says the feet of those messengers with good news, victory, and peace were a beautiful sight! Their beautiful feet were a sign that God is great! He saved His people!

Bibleman told the kids, "That's the good news the Bibleteam loves to share with you! The enemy is defeated! There is peace! Give thanks to Jesus! It's good news when you see my shoes of peace—part of the armor of God! I guess you can say I have beautiful feet! And so do you as you share the good news of Jesus with others!"

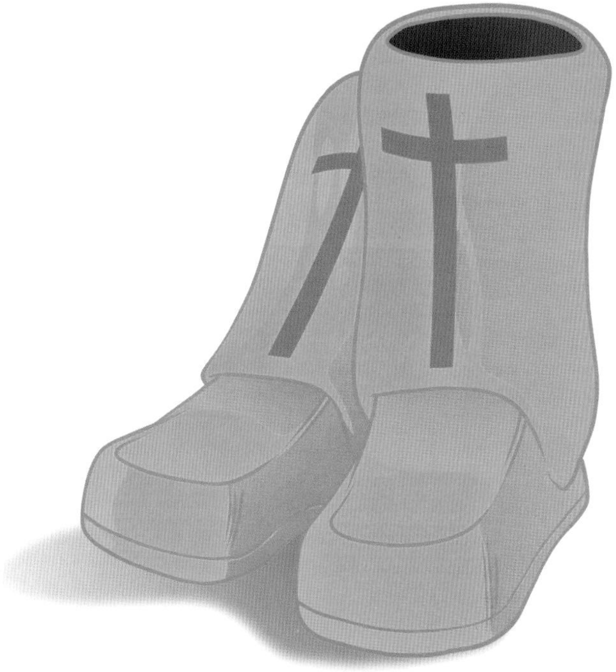

LET'S TALK

Who has God used as messengers in your life to share the good news of Jesus with you?

What different ways (words, songs, actions, TV, and others) have people shared God's Word and news with you?

With whom would you like to share the good news? What would you say?

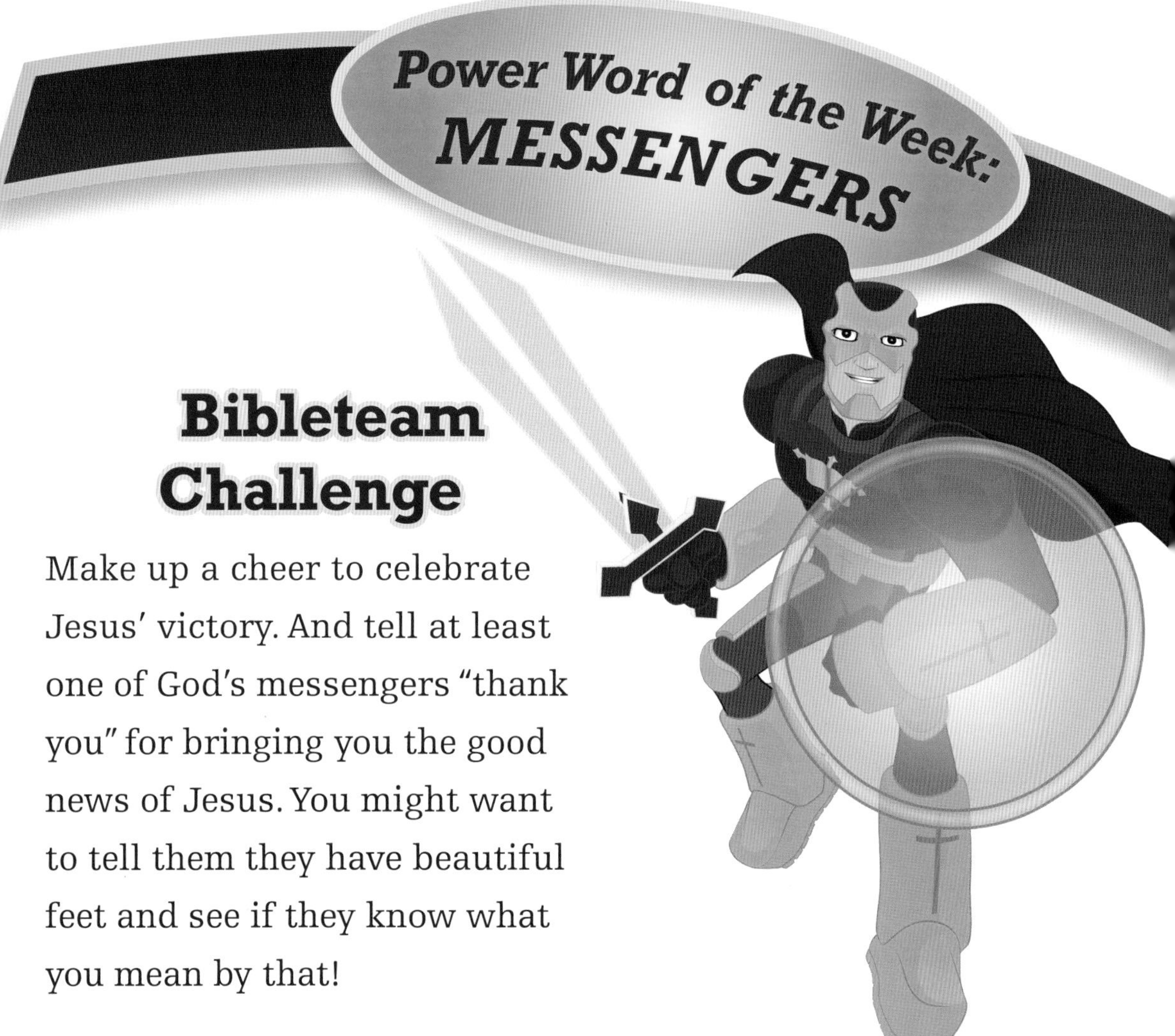

Bibleteam Challenge

Make up a cheer to celebrate Jesus' victory. And tell at least one of God's messengers "thank you" for bringing you the good news of Jesus. You might want to tell them they have beautiful feet and see if they know what you mean by that!

LET'S PRAY TOGETHER

Mighty Warrior, Jesus, thank You for winning the victory over sin and death for me. Thank You for the messengers who bring good news of Jesus to me and others. Amen.

Week 44

Prayer Warriors Take Down Enemies

Power Bible Verse

Pray constantly.
—1 Thessalonians 5:17

Mom, I heard you say Mrs. Litany is a prayer warrior. What does that mean?" Luis asked.

"A warrior is like a brave solider. One who fights for or against someone," she responded. "The Bibleteam members are warriors fighting to defeat the enemies. They fight for and with God's Word in the Bible. And they fight for us to make sure we keep trusting and following Jesus Christ. They use prayer in their fight too. They are prayer warriors."

"That's awesome, Mom!" Luis responded.

"Prayer warriors battle against enemies that want to hurt our trust in Jesus," Mom continued. "They battle through prayer. They love to pray. They pray and pray our enemies will stay away. They don't give up. Jesus knows and wants what is best for us. So they pray that God's best happens. They take down enemies and lift us up to Jesus. God's prayer warriors love God's Word and God's kids!"

"I want to be a prayer warrior too, like Mrs. Litany and the Bibleteam," Luis said excitedly. "It would be cool if others say about us, 'That's a family of prayer warriors on Team Jesus!'"

LET'S TALK

Who are some prayer warriors in your life?

Who are some of the people you prayed for this week? What did you pray about?

Where have you prayed this week?

Optional: Who do you pray for or what do you pray about the most? Why?

Power Word of the Week: PRAY

Bibleteam Challenge

Have someone help you make a list of people and things for which to pray. You may want to make a chart with your prayer list for every day of the week. Be ready to add to or change the list each week

LET'S PRAY TOGETHER

Dear Jesus, teach us to love praying for others like warriors, with You leading us! Amen.

Week 45

This Is the Day

Power Bible Verse

Rejoice in the Lord always.
I will say it again: Rejoice!
—Philippians 4:4

Cypher plopped down in his chair in the Bibleteam control room; he was tired. “Whew! We’ve been so busy fighting those mean villains I haven’t had time to clean up the control room,” Cypher sighed. “This is the day I’ll pick up the empty kiwi-lemon swirl slush-EZ cups Melody left here. This is the day I’ll work on new computer codes. And this is the day I’ll get my hair cut!”

Melody chimed in. “This is the day I’ll throw the kiwi-lemon swirl slush-EZ cup I drank from this morning in the trash,” she said, smiling at Cypher. “This is the day I’ll practice my gymnastics. And this is the day I’ll change the oil in the Biblevan.”

Biblegirl added, "This is the day I'll write some more Bible lessons for kids. This is the day I'll work on some new songs to use when we visit churches, schools, hospitals, and VBS classes. And this is the day I'll buy Cypher his favorite gross-sounding cantaloupe-bubblegum slush-EZ."

Bibleman had ideas too. "This is the day I'll polish my armor of God. This is the day I'll memorize more Bible verses to defeat enemies. This is the day we all come together, put down our slush-EZ, and happily shout together Psalm 118:24: Ready. Set. Go!"

"This is the day the LORD has made; let us rejoice and be glad in it," the entire team chanted together.

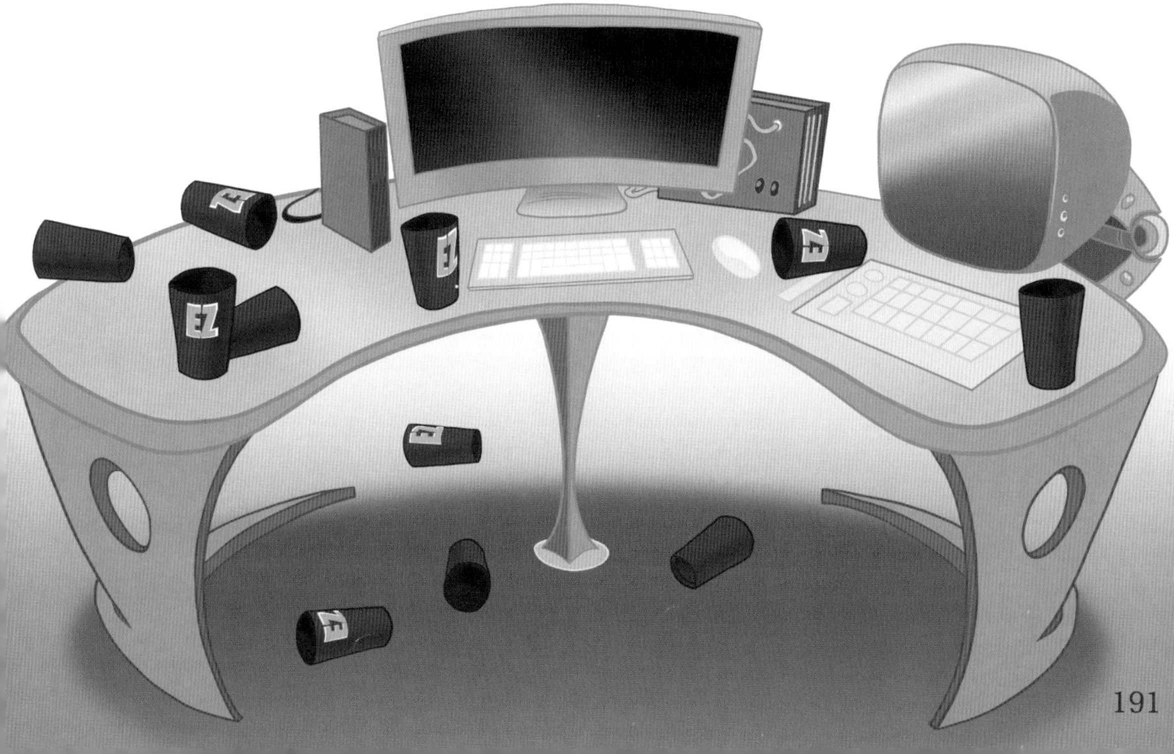

LET'S TALK

What are things that make you glad? What happened to make you rejoice today?

Finish this sentence: "This is the day I . . . ."

What has Jesus done for you that causes you to be glad and rejoice?

Optional: The Bibleteam has favorite drinks. What are yours?

Power Word of the Week: REJOICE

Bibleteam Challenge

Do or say something that might make someone else rejoice and be glad for one (or every) day this week. Also, memorize the words of Psalm 118:24—*This is the day the* LORD *has made; let us rejoice and be glad in it*—and say it every day this week.

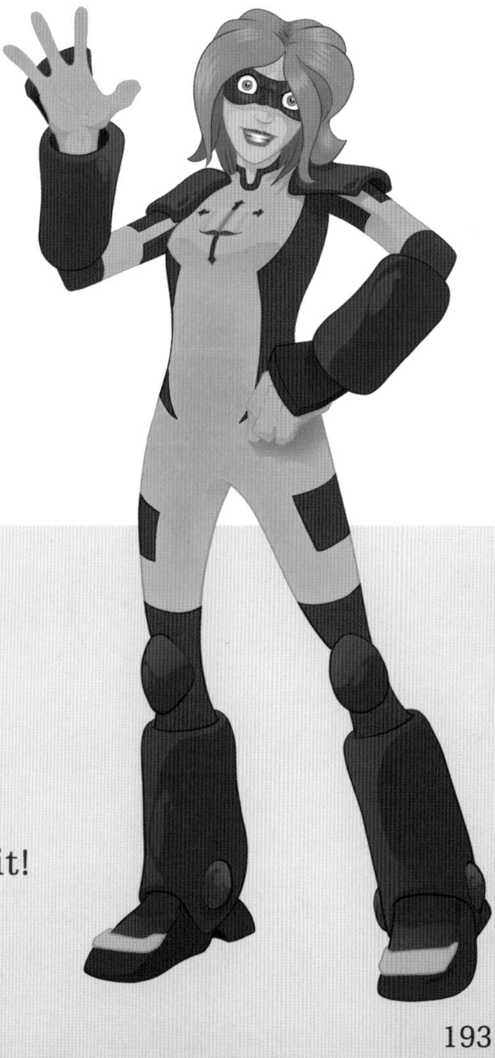

LET'S PRAY TOGETHER

Yes, Lord, this is the day You have made. I will rejoice and be glad in it! Amen.

Week 46

For Crying Out Loud, Empress!

Power Bible Verse

[Jesus] offered prayers and appeals with loud cries and tears.
—Hebrews 5:7

It didn't take long for the Empress of Unhappiness to get Franklin to cry. The Bibleteam arrived lickety-split! But the Empress had already left.

Franklin was embarrassed that the Bibleteam found him crying. He tried to stop, but the Empress had said some really mean and hurtful things. This was the third day in a row that Franklin had some things going on in his life that made him sad. He had a lot of tears to get out.

The Bibleteam made sure he knew that it's okay to cry! God created us with emotions and gave us tears to help us handle those sad and hurtful times. And sometimes tears come out because we're happy!

While Bibleman and Cypher went looking for the Empress, Biblegirl told Franklin that Jesus cried in front of other people too. He didn't hide it. When Jesus' friend Lazarus died, the Bible says in John 11:35–36, "Jesus wept. So the Jews said, 'See how he loved him!' Jesus understands what it's like to be sad and cry. And He's with you through both tears and smiles."

LET'S TALK

What are emotions, and what are some different emotions—good ones and ones that might be used in a bad way?

Why did God give us emotions?

How does it make you feel knowing Jesus cried?

Optional: When have you cried because you were happy? If you have never done that, what's the happiest thing you can think of that might cause you to cry tears of happiness? Ask your parents if they have ever cried when they were happy?

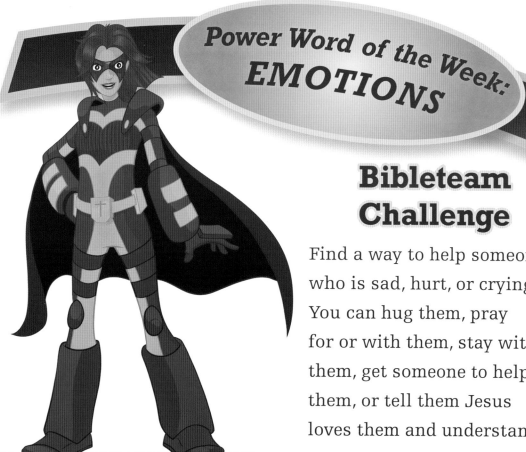

Power Word of the Week: EMOTIONS

Bibleteam Challenge

Find a way to help someone who is sad, hurt, or crying. You can hug them, pray for or with them, stay with them, get someone to help them, or tell them Jesus loves them and understands.

LET'S PRAY TOGETHER

Dear awesome God, thank You for creating emotions for our good. Thank You for the example of Jesus who showed His emotions. If any of my family or friends are sad and crying right now, make them feel better. Remind them You love them. And thank You for any family or friends who are so happy they could cry tears of joy. I'm so glad You're on my side. I pray in Jesus' name. Amen.

Week 47

No Sultan of Selfishness in Sight

Power Bible Verse

We love because he first loved us.
—1 John 4:19

The Bibleteam visited the kids at Grace N. Mercy Children's Hospital and shared smiles, encouraging Bible verses and stories, and the love of Jesus.

Cypher showed Elizabeth new gadgets and gizmos the Bibleteam uses. He put a floating laser message over her bed. It was Psalm 46:1: "God is our refuge and strength, a helper who is always found in times of trouble."

Biblegirl and Melody helped Michael put together a puzzle of Jesus smiling, with children around Him. And they sang a worship song with Michael's family.

Bibleman visited with Tyler. They talked about how to defeat villains like the Empress of Unhappiness, Dr. Fear, and the Mayor of Maybe. Bibleman asked, “If you could pray for one thing, what would it be?”

Tyler responded, “That my brother or sister never get sick like me.”

Wow! Bibleman thought Tyler would ask to be healed. He could have prayed for anything for himself, but his first thought was to pray for his brother and sister. Bibleman knew Tyler had such great love because Jesus first loved him. (And if the Sultan of Selfishness was around, he would have been knocked out by Tyler and his prayer!)

LET'S TALK

If you could pray for anything and anyone, what and who would it be? Is there any reason not to pray that prayer?

Tyler was unselfish, praying for his brother and sister. But it's also okay to pray for our own needs and problems. What would you like to pray for about yourself?

Psalm 46:1 says, "God is our refuge and strength, a helper who is always found in times of trouble." What does that mean to you? What is a refuge?

Optional: Ask your parents if you could bring Jesus' love to someone in the hospital.

Power Word of the Week: REFUGE

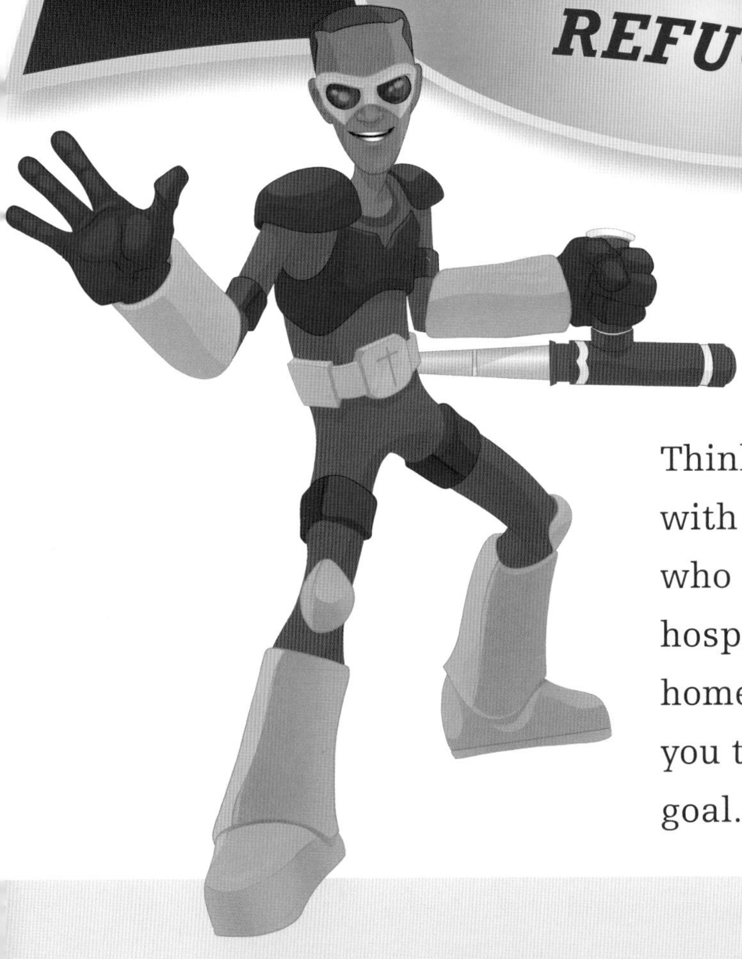

Bibleteam Challenge

Think of a way to reach out with Jesus' love to someone who is sick at home, in the hospital, or in the nursing home. Then ask your parents you to help accomplish your goal.

LET'S PRAY TOGETHER

Heavenly Father, thank You for the gift of prayer. I love knowing I can talk to You anytime and about anything. Please bless all who are sick at home or the hospital and those who take care of them. I pray they know You are with them and love them. I pray in the name of Jesus. Amen.

Week 48

Luxor's Messed-Up Worship Plan

Power Bible Verse

Jesus told him, "Go away, Satan! For it is written: Worship the Lord your God, and serve only him."
—Matthew 4:10

Luxor Spawndroth zapped Gayle and Albert with a disobey ray. They were confused and didn't recognize Luxor as he asked about Bibleman. Gayle and Albert told him Bibleman was a brave hero who battled enemies of God and led kids to Jesus with the Bible. Luxor said, "I never see Jesus, but I see Bibleman a lot. Maybe your pastor should change your church into the Bibleman Church. Sing Bibleman songs, worship him, pray to him—the great hero."

They heard a loud noise in the sky. Bibleman and Biblegirl were repelling down ropes from a helicopter. Bibleman jumped on Luxor and took him down, breaking his disobey ray gun.

Gayle and Albert told Biblegirl what Luxor said. Biblegirl shared a story from the book of Daniel that might have given Luxor the idea.

"King Nebuchadnezzar built a statue and made a law that everyone must worship it. Anyone who didn't would be thrown into a furnace of blazing fire. Three young men, Shadrach, Meshach, and Abednego, would not do it. They would only pray to and worship the one true God. They told the king, 'If the God we serve exists, then he can rescue us from the furnace of blazing fire' (Daniel 3:17). So they were thrown into the huge fire, but they were not hurt! The king was amazed and started to worship the one true God! Let's hope Luxor does the same."

LET'S TALK

What is the name of your church, and what does the name mean?

What is your favorite part of church and worshiping Jesus?

What is something you learned about Jesus in your church?

Optional: What did you learn about the story of Shadrach, Meshach, and Abednego? How does their decision help you as you live for Jesus?

Power Word of the Week: WORSHIP

Bibleteam Challenge

Thank your pastor for all that he does, especially for preaching and teaching the true Word of God. Pray for your pastor. Tell your pastor that you prayed for him.

LET'S PRAY TOGETHER

Lord, keep my faith strong to always trust and worship You. Thank You for my church, the pastors, teachers, and everyone who serves there. Help them to always share the truth of Your Word. Keep my faith strong so I will be like Shadrach, Meshach, and Abednego, always and only worshiping You. In Jesus' name. Amen.

Week 49
The Prince of Pride in an Upside Down World

Power Bible Verse

"For even the Son of Man did not come to be served, but to serve, and to give his life as a ransom for many."
—Mark 10:45

The first-grade class at Hope Christian School was excited that the Bibleteam came to lead them in their morning devotions. Cypher stood in front of the class and asked, "Do your feet smell?"

The kids laughed, and some said, "Yes!"

Melody asked, "Does your nose run?"

Most of the kids said theirs did.

Biblegirl said, "If your feet smell and your nose runs, I think you might be upside down! I run with my feet and smell with my nose!"

Bibleman told the kids, "Sometimes the Prince of Pride tries to cause trouble. He wants kids to think they are better than others. He likes when they brag that they're so great.

"Jesus' disciples, His close friends, argued one day about who was the greatest. Jesus turned their thinking upside down. Mark 9:35 says Jesus told them, 'If anyone wants to be first, he must be last and servant of all.'"

Biblegirl told the class that those words sounded backward and upside down! "To be first, we must be last. Who wants to be last? Who wants to serve? Many people don't. But people who give their lives to Jesus love helping others because Jesus first loved, served, and helped them!"

Then the team talked to kids about ways they could serve and help others. They decided it was fun living an upside-down kind of life!

LET'S TALK

How have you served or helped others this past week?

What are ways people served you last week?

What ways have you seen other people serve or help people?

What are some ways Jesus served others? What is the best way Jesus helped us?

Power Word of the Week: *SERVE*

Bibleteam Challenge

Think of ways you will serve other people this week. How and when will you do it? We don't help others to get thanks; we serve joyfully because Jesus first served us. But as you help others, notice how they act or what they say.

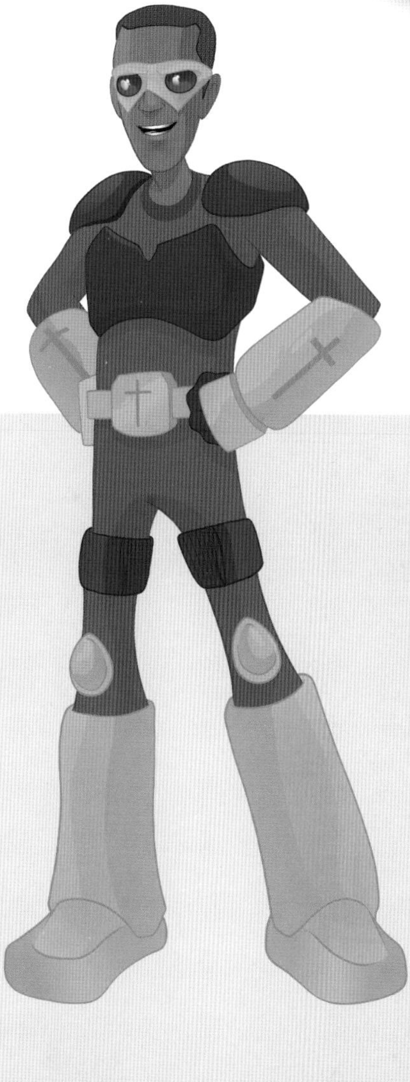

LET'S PRAY TOGETHER

Jesus, thank You for loving, serving, and helping me. That makes me want to do the same for others. Thank You for helping me in the best way ever by dying on the cross to forgive my sins and coming back alive to make it possible for me to live with You and all who love You in heaven forever. I love You! Amen.

Week 50

Slacker Fails the Fun Furrtill Family

Power Bible Verse

She will give birth to a son, and you are to name him Jesus, because he will save his people from their sins. —Matthew 1:21

Francesca and Gio let Slacker come to their house. Their mother was about to have a baby. Slacker didn't know she wanted the kids to make birth announcements or he wouldn't have come. He just wanted chips, fruit punch, and a TV to watch. But they wanted him to help.

He took paper from the recycling bin and said, "Just write that he's here. Then his name. Write that he looks like all babies. Then add, 'He likes Slacker because they both sleep, eat, and poop.' Tada! You're welcome. Where's the fruit punch?"

Melody happened to drop by to see if the baby had arrived. She saw Slacker and the look on Mrs. Furrtill's face. She knew she needed to get Slacker away from her kids. And that's what she did, telling Slacker about Jesus as they left!

Francesca said, "I wish we could have a birth announcement like God made when Jesus was born! Angels filled the sky! Our brother will be special, but there never was or will be a baby like Jesus! He was God's Son and Mary's son. He came to save the world from the mess of sin. Everyone in the world needs to know about perfect baby Jesus. We need to help tell them!"

LET'S TALK

What is your favorite part of the story of Jesus' birth?

Who were some people who first told you about the birth and life of Jesus?

What's your favorite Christmas song and the favorite thing your family does at Christmas?

Optional: What do you think about Slacker and the way he acted in the story? Have you ever acted like that?

Power Word of the Week: JESUS

Bibleteam Challenge

Thank as many people as you can think of who have told you about Jesus. You can thank them in person, with a card, an email, or maybe even a handmade gift.

LET'S PRAY TOGETHER

Jesus, Your birth and life changed the world and my life. Thank You for coming from heaven to earth because You love me. We needed You to rescue us from our sin. I want to tell the world everything about You. Amen.

Week 51

Everyone Loses at the Blame Game

Power Bible Verse

How joyful is the one whose transgression is forgiven, whose sin is covered!
—Psalm 32:1

Luxor knew Bibleman was following him around town, so he quickly threw a toxic blame gizmo into an open window where Pastor Eden and his family played a board game. Before long the Eden kids were arguing, playing the blame game: "She did it!" "He made me do it!" "Did not!" "She made me!" "Did not!" You get the idea.

Bibleman showed up at the door, but Pastor Eden said he'd take it from there. He told Bibleman to catch Luxor and run him out of town!

Pastor Eden reminded his family about when Adam and Eve sinned and the world went from perfect to broken.

They played the blame game too. Pastor Eden told them everyone sins, but we need to stop blaming others and admit what we have done. Thankfully, God sent Jesus to clean up our sinful mess. The Apostle Paul wrote in 2 Corinthians 5:21: "He made the one who did not know sin to be sin for us, so that in him we might become the righteousness of God."

In the blame game, everyone loses. So, the Eden kids all took turns forgiving each other before getting back to their board game and some family fun.

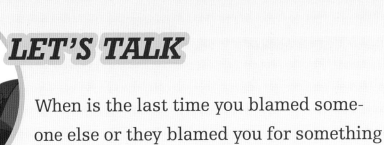

LET'S TALK

When is the last time you blamed someone else or they blamed you for something you did? How did it make you feel?

The key verse uses the big word *transgression*. That's another word for sin. How does it make you feel knowing Jesus forgives your sins? How do you feel when you forgive someone for something they did wrong to you?

What does it mean that Jesus is blameless?

Optional: What is a favorite game you play with your family?

Power Word of the Week: BLAMELESS

Bibleteam Challenge

Plan to play a game with your family this week. Try to make sure you have fun together!

LET'S PRAY TOGETHER

Dear Jesus, please take care of our family. Help us to love and forgive each other. Thank You for saving us from the big mess our sin got us into. You took the blame for us. I love Your love. Amen.

Week 52

Goodbye, Ambassador; Amen, Jesus!

Power Bible Verse

The grace of the Lord Jesus be with everyone. Amen.
—Revelation 22:21

The Ambassador of Ignorance planned to make Joey think he wasn't smart, even though he was. He teased him, "You don't know the last word in the Bible. You don't know what word sounds the same in almost every language in the world. You probably don't know what it means, Joey! And you—"

Bibleman burst into the room before the Ambassador could say another word. Bibleman spoke kindly to Joey, saying, "Jesus has all the answers for your life and mine." Bibleman talked to him about the love of Jesus, who rescues us from sin and life without God, about forgiveness, and all His heavenly gifts He gives freely. "It's never too late—"

But the Ambassador flew out of the room before Bibleman could finish. Joey and Bibleman were disappointed, but they hoped one day the Ambassador would put his trust in Jesus.

"By the way, Joey. The answer to his questions is the word Amen," Bibleman explained. "*Amen* is a powerful word that means *Yes! I agree! This is true!"* What a perfect last word for the Bible in Revelation 22:21. What a great way to end our prayers!"

Joey replied, "Amen to that, Bibleman. I'm glad you came to help me and teach me about Jesus and His words. Amen. Amen. Amen!"

Amen!

LET'S TALK

The Ambassador of Ignorance didn't believe or trust in Jesus as his rescuer from sin and the way to heaven. Who are some people you know who don't believe in Jesus? In what ways can you share Jesus' love and words with them?

Write the meaning of the word *amen*.

This week's key verse is the last verse in the Bible. Grace is love that we don't deserve, and there's nothing we can do to earn it. It's a gift. Re-read the key verse. Why is that a good way to end the Bible?

Bibleteam Challenge

This week when you pray and say amen, say or think about the meaning of that word. Also, make a list of people to pray for who don't believe or trust in Jesus. Keep the list so you can remember to pray for them.

LET'S PRAY TOGETHER

Amen, Jesus! Thank You for loving me, teaching me Your ways and words. Please bring all my family, friends, and even my enemies to know of Your love and trust in You. I love You! Amen and Amen!

Remember:

Your word is a lamp for my feet and a light on my path.—Psalm 119:105

Read:

The Bible is filled with verses about Bible study. Romans 15:4 says that everything written in the past was written for us to learn from it. God wants us to learn from His Word, and the best way to do that is to spend time with it. Joshua 1:8 tells us to always be reading, thinking about, and studying God's Word so that we can understand and obey God.

You see, God gave us the Bible to help guide us through life and to let us know how best to live for Him. That is why Psalm 119:105 calls God's Word a lamp and a light—it shows us the way in an otherwise dark or uncertain world. And the best part is that even though the Bible was written thousands of years ago, it is still true and meaningful today. Hebrews 4:12 tells us "the word of God is alive and active." The Bible will always be a great place to find God's love and wisdom no matter what happens in the world or how old the Bible is.

Think:

Name a devotion that helped you learn about God and the way He wants you to live.

1. Why do you think God wants us to study the Bible?
2. Who can you ask to help you understand the Bible?
3. How does obeying God's Word make your life better?
4. How many Bible verses can you find about studying the Bible?

Do:

Make a plan for your devotional time. Talk with your parents about setting a time each week, or even each day, to do a devotion together. Mark your devotion time on a calendar, and ask your parents to set a reminder or alarm so you don't forget. You can even write on your calendar which verse or Bible passage you're going to study.

During your devotions, remember to ask questions if you don't understand something. End each devotional time by talking about how you can use what you learned the next day. Pray that God will help you to remember and show what you learned.